'Keep your han

'Is *that* what you wa
was heavy with feign
me, Linnet! I could have sworn that you . . . well, never mind.'

'*You* may take it for granted that women find you irresistible, but I, for one, do not go around looking for sexual harrassment!' Linnet snapped icily. 'You misunderstood me—misinterpreted me—quite deliberately back there, and you know it!'

Dear Reader

With the long summer evenings, what better way to relax than by reading a selection of stories which really take you away from it all? With four exciting contemporary romances, Mills & Boon will transport you to some of the most exotic locations in the world. Enjoy the luxury of those places you always wanted to visit... surely the perfect chance to dream of your ideal man! Look out for our summer packs in your local shops or contact our Reader Service and indulge yourself in the world of romance!

The Editor

Lee Stafford was born and educated in Sheffield where she worked as a secretary, and later as a public relations assistant. However, she has been a compulsive scribbler for as long as she can remember. She lives in Sussex with her husband, their two teenage daughters and three cats. To keep fit, she swims and does a weekly dance-exercise class. When not travelling to research new backgrounds, she likes to relax at the small apartment they recently bought in France.

Recent titles by the same author:

SHADOW IN THE WINGS
SUMMER'S ECHO
A HEART DIVIDED

THE WILLING CAPTIVE

BY

LEE STAFFORD

MILLS & BOON LIMITED
ETON HOUSE, 18-24 PARADISE ROAD
RICHMOND, SURREY TW9 1SR

First published in Great Britain 1993
by Mills & Boon Limited

This edition 1993

ISBN 0 263 78080 5

Set in Times Roman 10 on 12 pt.
01-9307-54606 C

Made and printed in Great Britain

CHAPTER ONE

SHE had arrived like a princess—which was only fitting, Linnet thought apprehensively, considering the style and splendour of her destination. The water-taxi had picked her up at exactly the appointed time from her quietly luxurious hotel fronting the Grand Canal, and conveyed her, gaping openly at historic churches and palaces, along its sinuously curving journey through the heart of Venice.

All manner of craft churned up the busy waters: honking *vaporetti*, the everyday transport of Venetians going about their business, gondoliers skilfully plying their touristic trade in elegant, traditional craft, barges delivering vegetables to canal-side markets. Brightly awninged cafés with tables at the water's edge were already alive with well-dressed people drinking coffee. It was all as she had imagined it, or seen it in countless pictures, only more so. Much, much more.

And then her anxiety, briefly overcome by her fascination with the sights and sounds all around her, had returned as the taxi had turned off the main thoroughfare down a quieter canal, lined by tall, elegantly secretive houses, where even the ripple of the water seemed subdued, and drew up at a private landing-stage with a short flight of marble steps leading up to a splendid door of dark wood inlaid with panels of brass and silver.

Linnet's breath came quickly as she alighted, endeavouring to make the transition from bobbing boat to firm ground as gracefully as possible. There was nothing for her to pay—all that, like her flight and her hotel, had been taken care of.

The doors were opened to her as by a pre-arranged signal, and she had only just time to register a swift, fleeting impression of dusky pink walls and tall windows decoratively picked out by arched friezes of white brickwork, before following a gravely smiling man-servant into the sumptuous marble-floored hall.

Here she was! The Ca' Favorita. The lion's lair. And all too soon she would have to face this particular lion, somehow retaining her calm, concealing the seething hatred that even now was boiling up again inside her for Maximiliano di Angeli, the rich, spoiled international playboy who had ruined Joanna's life.

Dear Joanna, Linnet's childhood idol, reduced to a wrung-out, nervous shadow of her former vivacious self by her treatment at this man's hands, and dying uselessly, before she was thirty, in an horrific, head-on car crash. It was all *his* fault, this man whom she was about to meet for the first time, but already fiercely detested. Having married Joanna, all he'd had to do was love her. It couldn't have been hard; she was funny and smart, as well as beautiful.

Linnet choked back the angry lump in her throat. This would not do. He must not be allowed to guess at or somehow pick up her hostile feelings, or she would be out on her ear, and then she would never learn the truth of what had happened. She was just a girl who had applied for a job. A girl who knew nothing about him, except that he needed someone who spoke English to help care for his small daughter.

'*Signorina*?'

The servant led her through the hall into an equally impressive drawing-room, where softly glowing oriental rugs partly covered the marble. There were chandeliers of ornate Murano glass suspended from a ceiling which looked as if it had been painted by Tiepolo. And that was almost certainly an original Canaletto on the wall facing her.

Overawed by her surroundings, and fighting to master her nervousness, Linnet, left alone, sank gracefully on to a damask-covered chair which looked like a museum exhibit, but was surprisingly comfortable. Across the room, she caught sight of her reflection in a gilt-framed mirror, and was startled by its incongruity—a wraith-slim girl, narrow-waisted and long-legged, with a fall of straight fair hair well below her shoulders, eyes large and wide in her pale face. Anyone could see that she did not belong here, among this baroque magnificence. A strong desire to jump up and run seized her, and an irrational suspicion that the great outer doors would be barred, preventing her escape, filled her with the panic-stricken sensation of being a prisoner.

It was a very ordinary sound which saved her, a childish voice, high and piping, with echoes of school playgrounds from long ago.

'Tinker, tailor, soldier, sailor...'

The voice petered out, to pick up the refrain a moment later. 'Tinker, tailor...'

Her eyes following the direction from which it came, Linnet saw what, lost in the splendours around her, she had failed to notice before. At the far end of the spacious room, full-length glass doors opened on to a small patio garden, stone-flagged, with a sparkling central fountain, small trees, and tubs of brilliant flowers. A little girl was playing out there, all alone, with a skipping rope, in a world of her own, chanting a rhyme that generations of English children had learned.

Excitement quickened Linnet's pulse. This had to be Joanna's daughter Cassie. She shouldn't, really, she knew... but an aching curiosity stronger than she could contain brought her to her feet, and she tiptoed softly across the marble acres to the open glass doors.

'Tinker, tailor...' The small skipper, no more than five years old, stopped, her face wrinkling with concentration. Her bobbed hair was a rich, dark brown, but she had Joanna's exquisite straight nose. Linnet clasped her hands, combating an unbearable wave of mingled sadness and joy, and her movement alerted the child, who turned to gaze at her with fearless innocence, Joanna's insouciant smile curving the soft young lips.

'*Ciao. Come ti chiami*?' she demanded cheerily.

'My name is Linnet,' Linnet replied automatically in English, and the child's grin widened.

'Linnet—like a bird?' she said clearly in the same. 'That's a funny name for a girl—but I like it. I'm called Cassie—that's really short for Cosima.'

Linnet smiled. Maybe she would not get the job, and these few minutes were all she would ever have of Joanna's child. Fighting back a desire to cry, she said, 'I used to play that skipping game when I was little, you know.'

Cassie frowned. 'I forgot the words,' she confessed.

'I know them,' Linnet said. 'Tinker, tailor, soldier, sailor, rich man, poor man, beggar man, thief...'

Giggling delightedly, Cassie took up the chant and began to skip. 'Can you run in?' she called. The years fell away from Linnet, and in seconds they were skipping and chanting together, a little clumsily, owing to the difference in their heights, and both of them laughing.

A slow, measured handclap caught them unawares and, stopping self-consciously, Linnet found her ankles tangled in the rope, while Cassie, still giggling, collapsed against her.

'Papà! Linnet can skip very well—but she is too big for me!'

The man was leaning negligently against the doorframe. He was very tall—at least six feet three, at a guess, but in no sense of the word gangling, because this height was matched by a suitable breadth of shoulder and chest, and although he wore a dark suit, with the long, elegant jacket unbuttoned, there was a discreet suggestion of muscle defined beneath it. His hair was black and sleeked back from a patrician brow, his mouth curved in a condescending amusement. His eyes were startlingly blue—almost gentian—and Linnet was uncomfortably sure their laziness was entirely deceptive.

'*Bravissimo*, Miss Halsey. It is Miss Halsey, I assume?'

The dark velvet voice reassured her no more than had the casual gaze. She was willing to bet that both of them were a front, and behind them lurked a steely, ruthless persona. For this had to be him—the man, the villain of her imagination—and here she was, being caught doing something silly, behaving like a schoolgirl, her face flushed, hair straying from one of the clips which had anchored it behind her ear. Linnet extricated her feet carefully from the tangle of skipping-rope and pushed back the long blonde strand with a nervous gesture.

'I'm Max di Angeli,' he said easily, without giving her a chance to speak. He did not offer her his hand, but indicated with it that she should return indoors, displaying a smooth authority which made Linnet feel as if she had been apprehended out of bounds. 'Shall we go into the drawing-room?'

'Me, too, Papà!' Cassie piped up.

He dropped swiftly to his haunches, resting his hands on the small shoulders.

'No, not you, *piccola*. I have to talk to Miss Halsey on my own. You go back to Aunty Dina now, and I shall come and see you soon.'

Cassie obeyed, although reluctantly. Not even his daughter would argue too seriously with this man, Linnet thought darkly. To be fair, she had not sensed any fear in the child—but even the worst criminals loved and were loved by their children, she told herself briskly. It meant nothing.

Once again she found herself seated in the damask chair, but now he was opposite her, long legs stretched out and crossed at the ankles, hands resting lightly on the chair arms. Totally relaxed, but as a cat rested, ready always to spring alert if need be. A predator of a man.

'You appear to enjoy the company of children—and their games,' he said, in a soft drawl, and Linnet's flush deepened. He seemed to be insinuating that she was immature, and surely he would not employ anyone he did not consider responsible?

'I enjoy the company of people. Children are people too,' she countered quietly.

An almost imperceptible flicker of surprise gleamed in the blue eyes.

'So?' he said. It was half-question, half-statement. Linnet moistened her lips. She was suddenly beset by serious doubts about the impulse which had propelled her into applying for this job. It was not merely whether she *wanted* to work for this man and live in his house, but whether she even *dared*. He frightened her, and she was convinced he would see through her. If Joanna, who could cope magnificently with anything male, had been destroyed by him, what hope was there for her?

Joanna had been in love with him—you aren't, she reminded herself. All the same...

'I like children,' she said, 'but I've never worked with them. I'm not a nanny, a nurse, a teacher, or qualified in any way.'

'Such honesty,' he murmured, suddenly shifting his stance, draping one leg elegantly across the other, and half leaning towards her. 'One might think you were trying to talk yourself *out* of a job, not *into* it. What is it, I wonder, that has made you go cold on the idea? Don't you like Venice? Don't you like my house... my daughter? Or perhaps it is myself...?'

The lapis lazuli eyes rested on her, contemplative and indolent, not at all concerned by the latter possibility. Why indeed should it worry him? He was rich and undeniably handsome, and Linnet was sure he had women leaping at him in hordes.

'It's nothing of the sort,' she contradicted swiftly. 'Venice is fascinating, your house is magnificent, and your daughter is enchanting. And I hardly know you, *signore*. But it would be wrong of me to pretend to be what I am not.'

'Foolish, too. I would expect such claims to be backed up by evidence,' he said imperturbably. 'No matter—it is not important. I already employ sundry teachers of music, dancing and so forth. My daughter is surrounded by people who care for her and look after her welfare. But they all speak mostly in Italian, and I want... a companion... who will speak to her in English. Her mother, who was English, died recently, and I do not wish Cosima to lose her fluency in the language.'

His bald statement of his wife's death, with its implication that his child's greatest loss would be her ability to speak her maternal tongue, took Linnet's breath away.

No wonder Joanna had chain-smoked until the ends of her fingers were yellowed, and drunk more than was good for her. 'I'm nothing to Max,' she had declared with a low-keyed, frightening anger. 'One woman is as good as another, to him.' Obviously he had ceased to care for her long ago, and she had borne his indifference only for Cassie's sake, until finally even that link had snapped under the strain.

He was still regarding her steadily, and Linnet realised she had to say something.

'You speak English extremely well yourself, *signore,*' she said. 'I would hardly have thought Cassie needed any further help.

He acknowledged this fact without unnecessary modesty. 'But I am away a great deal,' he pointed out. 'To a child, continuity is vital.'

Then don't be, she wanted to retort. Stay for Cassie, as you would not do for her mother. Leave the jet-setting, the skiing and surfing, the parties and the women, at least for the years of her childhood. But she could hardly say it.

'I see,' was all she replied, primly and with a hint of reproach that elicited another swift flash of amusement from those astounding eyes.

'Do you? I wonder.' He got up, prowled across the room, then turned, looking like a lawyer in a courtroom, about to cross-examine. 'Motivation,' he said suddenly. 'Why are you here? Or, to put it another way, if you were not here, what else would you be doing?'

Once again Linnet was left breathless, but this time by his shrewdness. Playboy he might be, but he was an unconventional one. A needle-sharp brain ticked away relentlessly beneath that handsome exterior.

'I would be here in Italy, but to study under Maestro Donetti,' she said, this time utterly truthful and absolutely herself.

His eyebrows arched with sharp interest. 'The famous music teacher? You are a singer, then?' he demanded.

She nodded. 'Yes. At least, I trained to be, and hope one day to resume that training. I was ill...I had to have an operation on my vocal cords earlier this year, and I was told not to sing—not properly, anyhow—until a year from that time.'

She spoke briskly, unsentimentally, not wishing to reveal the heartache this had caused her, or to appear to be seeking this man's pity.

'My condolences, *signorina*.' His sympathetic response seemed real, but could have been mere politeness. 'So you decided that, if you could not sing, at least you could be here in Italy?'

Linnet swallowed. Yes, but she had not truly realised that, not until yesterday when she had stepped off the plane into the golden Italian sunshine, and heard the music of the language all around her. Not until she'd seen the pigeons wheeling high above the Piazza San Marco, heard the gondoliers calling tunefully to one another, and seen, from her hotel terrace, the sunset over the lagoon, with the island of San Giorgio Maggiore etched black against it. Then it had come rushing at her, how much of the music of Verdi and Puccini and Donizetti, which she had so loved to sing, was bound up with the aura, the landscape of this ravishing country. Italy was an operatic backdrop. Its reality had sung in the veins of the great composers, and a small part of it lived in her.

'I suppose...' she said with a frown, momentarily forgetting how she hated Max di Angeli, thinking only how strange it was that he should understand this. Looking up at him, she saw that he had caught the uncertainty in her, and she thought, I can kiss goodbye to this. She remembered Cassie, and was suddenly sad. Never mind how she felt about her father, she could have loved that child.

He continued to study her, his expression thoughtful but unrevealing; however, in his very stillness, Linnet sensed dissatisfaction.

'You are very young,' he said disparagingly, 'and I expect you are going to be frightfully honest again, and admit you don't understand Italian, which is the language most of my household speaks, not surprisingly.'

Linnet was aware of a rising irritation, and suddenly she ceased to care whether this man approved of her or not. He wasn't going to offer her the job, and she could walk out of here and never see him again.

'I shall be twenty-two very shortly, and there is no way I could add any more years to that, if I wanted to,' she said, with a touch of sharpness. 'As a matter of fact, I *understand* quite a bit of Italian—most operatic libretti were written in it—although speaking it well might take me a little time. However, I can see I'm not what you want, so I won't waste any more of your time, or my own!'

She had risen to her feet with her last words, but before she could set off on the long walk across the marble floors he was at her side, his hand on her arm—not holding it, but restraining her with the lightest touch, fingers merely brushing her skin.

Her expected reaction of horror and revulsion did not come, but before she had the chance to analyse why his touch was not unpleasant to her he had removed his hand.

'Sit down, Miss Halsey. Please,' he said quietly. She stood where she was for a full half-minute, silently resisting him. He did not move, simply gestured eloquently towards the chair, and Linnet's defiance crumbled. She sank mutely to the seat, a deep sense of the irrevocable slowly enveloping her.

'That's better,' he said approvingly. 'We Italians appreciate a little temperament, but please don't try to outplay us at our own game.'

A vestigial smile lightened the corners of his mouth, and Linnet could not help but be aware of how disturbingly attractive he was—really, there was no point in denying the fact, however one felt about him. He had a powerful charm, which he used as just one weapon in his well-equipped armory, and she could see how easily a woman might succumb to it, if she were not forewarned.

'I only play games with children, *signore*,' she said.

'I saw you doing that, remember,' he replied, and Linnet flushed again, sure her face must resemble a peony. 'The point in your favour, Miss Halsey, is that Cosima appears to have taken to you. So, under certain conditions, the position is yours.'

Linnet almost jumped in her chair; her hands clutched the smoothly curved arms. She had not expected this; even when he had called her back, she had imagined she was only in for a lecture, and now she was in a nervous dilemma. She wanted this, didn't she? Or did she? It certainly did not seem to have occurred to him that *she* might of her own accord turn it down, but she supposed he was not accustomed to rejection on any level. He was Max di Angeli, favourite of European high society, in demand in half a dozen capitals and on everyone's country estate.

'C-conditions?' she stammered foolishly, still unsure of how to react.

'To begin,' he said, 'I would want you to stay for a short trial period—say, two weeks—to see how you settled down in the household, and with Cosima. After that, if I were satisfied with you, I would require you to commit yourself for a period of six months.'

Linnet gasped.

'You mean I would have to sign a contract?' she demanded.

'Of course.' His gaze was hard, unyielding. 'When Cosima is six, she will be starting her full-time education at a very special school, where much of the tuition will be in English. It will then be less crucial what she speaks at home. Until that time, I want this role to be filled by the same person. Cosima needs stability, especially now. I can't have her upset by continual changes.'

She licked her lips. 'And is this six-month contractual obligation intended to be binding on your side also?'

His laugh was humourless. 'Naturally not. If you ceased to be satisfactory, for any reason, I would have to leave myself the option of being able to dismiss you.'

'It's a little unfair,' she cavilled.

'Perhaps,' he conceded imperturbably. 'But that's the way it must be. However, I won't ask you to make a snap decision this very minute.' His glance flew to the ornate, cherub-gilded clock as if already his attention was elsewhere. 'I have another appointment very soon. By this evening, you will have made up your mind.'

It wasn't a question. In fact, the whole arrangement smacked of extreme arrogance on his part. Notwithstanding his natural concern for his daughter, all the rights would be on his side, and none on hers, once she accepted. He could be the most demanding and unpleasant of employers, and she would not even have the elementary last resort of walking out!

Was this how he had made Joanna's life a misery? Had his wife been little more than a prisoner, obliged to agree to his demands and make none in return? Linnet shivered, and the pendulum of her own desires swung violently against having anything to do with Max di Angeli on any level.

'I won't need that long,' she said promptly.

'Nevertheless, you will *take* that long,' he insisted with quiet emphasis. 'Do nothing in haste, or swayed by emotion of any kind, is a good dictum, Miss Halsey.'

At this, her head went up, and she stared at him, unable to hide her astonishment. What exactly did he mean? What emotions had he discerned in her, in this short interview?

He laughed, amused by her consternation. 'It isn't necessary that you like *me*, you know,' he said, and his unconcerned awareness of her aversion threw her into a deep embarrassment.

'As I've said, I don't know you,' she muttered, and the soft laugh rippled across her nerves yet again.

'You don't have to, do you?' he countered. And then, unexpectedly, 'quite close to your hotel, in the Calle Vallaresso, there's a place called Harry's Bar. It's where Ernest Hemingway used to drink when he lived here, if you're interested in literary associations. Meet me there tonight, at eight.' Another glance at the clock. 'I have to go now. Gianni will call you a water-taxi.'

Without another word, he strode off in the direction of the patio where earlier she had skipped with Cassie, leaving Linnet speechless, outraged and puzzled all at once. Just before he reached the glass doors, he turned and over his shoulder he casually called, '*Ciao*,' and then he was gone, disappearing behind the ferns and shrubs and presumably through another door beyond them.

Linnet saw none of the glories of Venice on her journey back to the hotel. She sat bolt upright in the water-taxi, staring blindly ahead, her mind and her senses full of the Ca' Favorita . . . but, even more so, of its owner.

'I hate that man!' Joanna had declared, curled up as if seeking protection in the window-seat of the library of Verne Hall, her parental home in the green depths of the Sussex countryside. 'I must have been insane to have married him,' she had continued in a flat, distraught monotone, lighting a cigarette from the stub of her last. 'He never loved me. I doubt he has ever loved any woman. He's incapable of love!'

This had been earlier in the year, when the lifeless trees had just begun, tentatively, to unfurl new buds, but a chill March wind had whipped their branches. Linnet, still convalescing from the major operation on her vocal cords which had cast a blight on her glowing future, was not supposed to venture out in the cold, but after an imperiously heart-rending phone call from the newly returned Joanna she had bundled herself up warmly, borrowed her parents' car, and driven over to the Hall.

'Oh, but Joanna!' Linnet had cried, recalling the radiant girl who had gone out to Italy as a bride seven years earlier. 'It was so wonderful—like a fairy-tale! Surely you must still love each other?'

'A fairy-tale is all it ever was, Linnet,' Joanna had remarked sourly. 'Oh, I can't expect you to understand, mouse. You've never been married, and at a guess you're still pretty naïve about men. Besides, it's different for you. You've got a brilliant career ahead of you.'

'Not now, I haven't,' Linnet had been obliged to remind her quietly, smiling a little wryly at Joanna's use of the childhood nickname she herself had given the younger girl.

'What? Oh, yes, Mummy did say something about your op... but once you've healed up you can pick up where you left off, can't you?'

Linnet had shaken her head at Joanna's easy assumption that her problems would be so easily solved. She had been expressly forbidden to sing for a full year, and who knew, until then, what permanent damage her voice might have suffered, or if, indeed, it would be the same voice? Or if Maestro Donetti would still feel able to offer her a place on his prestigious scholarship scheme? It was not simple.

But Joanna hadn't understood any of that, she had reminded herself guiltily; she knew nothing about music, or the rigours of operatic training. What was more, her marriage seemed to be tragically breaking up. Linnet could have kicked herself for letting her own troubles intrude on Joanna's sorrow. That was not why she had come over.

'I'll manage,' she had said stoically, patting the other girl's hand. 'But what about you? What are *you* going to do?'

'God knows,' Joanna had said bleakly, tossing back a full measure of Scotch in one swallow. Three weeks later, she was dead.

The day of the funeral was bitterly cold, and Linnet's doctors had expressly forbidden her to attend it, so she had not been at the graveside in the local churchyard to see the coffin being lowered into the Verne family vault. But nothing could have stopped her from going over to the Hall, afterwards, to pay her respects along with the other mourners.

'Where is Joanna's husband?' she had murmured to Lady Verne, her eyes scanning the subdued group of people for a sight of the mysterious Italian.

Lady Verne had shaken her head disapprovingly.

'He was here briefly, for the service and the interment, but he would not stay any longer,' she said tautly. 'He didn't bring the child either—can you imagine? In my opinion, she should come to live with us—after all, she's half English, and without a mother—but he won't hear of it. Says he wants her to remain in her own home. She might visit us, perhaps, when she is older. I'm inclined to contest that, you know, see if we could get custody.'

Linnet was not surprised. Lady Verne had always been a bossy, domineering woman who liked her own way.

'I do understand how you feel,' she said sympathetically. 'But it would be difficult... he *is* her father.'

'Huh.' Lady Verne was haughtily dismissive. 'Have you seen what he's doing?' She showed Linnet a small, discreet advertisement in a top people's magazine. 'Advertising for someone to look after my granddaughter! The idea of it!'

Linnet murmured something soothing and made her escape. She had found Lady Verne frightening enough as a child, when she had been a member of the local guide troop which Joanna's mother, as the incumbent of the 'big house', had run. That was how she had first got to know Joanna. Several years her senior, Joanna had casually bestowed her attention on Linnet, and had received in return the younger girl's adoration. Joanna had possessed a carefree beauty. She swam like a fish, danced like a dream, rode like a Valkyrie. She did most things well and effortlessly. Linnet, in those days, was a thin, pale little thing, well deserving, so she thought, of the careless epithet 'mouse'. She never knew why Joanna bothered with her, but she was grateful for it. She had no claim to any sort of excellence herself until later, when she discovered the full glory of her own voice.

By then, Joanna was going around with Rupert Morton, whose family owned a large neighbouring farm. The couple were seen everywhere together, and it was universally assumed that they would marry. It didn't happen. All of a sudden, out of the blue, so it seemed to Linnet, Joanna was to marry this blue-blooded Italian whose lineage was thick with the famous names of European nobility. He was the catch of the year, and somehow Joanna had netted him.

'Jo should have married me,' Rupert had said to Linnet at the funeral. 'I understood her. It would have been better.'

There was nothing she could sensibly have replied. In truth, she had been surprised even to see him there. His family had moved away from the area a year or two after Joanna married, and Linnet had not seen him since. She had supposed that he and Joanna must have lost touch, but somehow he had turned up, looking pale and grief-stricken, so it seemed that after all these years he must still care.

Driving home from Verne Hall, she remembered the advertisement Lady Verne had shown her, and that was when the idea first came to her. She wanted to know what had gone wrong, what that awful man had done to her beloved Joanna, and here was a way to find out.

She had answered the advertisement, using the London address where she had lived while studying at the Royal College of Music, where the girls she had shared with still sent on her mail. That way, she preserved her anonymity and avoided any connection with Joanna's part of the country. She had tried not to let her hopes carry her away—there must be any number of young women who would relish the opportunity to spend some time in Italy, living in a Venetian palazzo, no less, so why should she even reach the short-list?

But the summons had come, and with it her air ticket and hotel booking, and there was no turning back. She had set her foot on this path, and she knew she had to follow it through, wherever it led.

It had led her here, she reflected, gazing out of her hotel window at the rippling waves of the Grand Canal, with the flamboyant domes and buttresses of Santa Maria della Salute outlined against blue sky and blue water. It had led her to a decision she must now make entirely alone.

The easiest thing would be to tell Max di Angeli that she had, after consideration, decided to decline his offer, and to high-tail it back to England. Her crazy impulse had been fuelled by a need to unravel the threads of Joanna's tragedy, to learn why it had happened as it had. But what would she learn from living at the Ca' Favorita that she could not already guess? Max was a charming, high-handed, unscrupulous rogue who had been born with too much of everything, and expected more. Being a faithful and devoted husband to one woman was not his style.

Long before she met him, Linnet had been predisposed to hate him, but the reality was harder and more complex. He scared her. He was out of her league, a man from another world, a world of wealth, influence and luxury completely alien and unknown to her. She was afraid to move into his orbit, into this kingdom he ruled with such arrogance, and even to contemplate it brought on an attack of that panic-filled sense of being a prisoner that had assailed her at the Ca' Favorita.

'I can't do it,' she said aloud to the listening silence of her room. It was no use. She would tell him tonight that she was very sorry, but she could not accept his offer.

Coward, said an accusing inner voice, and Linnet, bowing her head, admitted the truth of this condemnation. Defeat written in every line of her slender body, she began to get ready for her appointment with Max di Angeli.

CHAPTER TWO

CALLE VALLARESSO was one of a number of narrow streets which led down to the Grand Canal, and Harry's Bar was right at the end, a stone's throw from a station where gondolas were moored and *vaporetti* disgorged passengers.

The May evening was still bright and warm, and full daylight, and Linnet had walked the short distance from her hotel. Smart, stylish Venetians were going out for an evening's pleasure, restaurants and bars were busy, shops still open, and terrace tables were rapidly filling up, waiters dashing in and out, balancing trays with skilful aplomb.

Harry's Bar was not at all what Linnet had expected. It was not a conventional continental bar at all; there were no outside tables, just one discreet door, and the glass in the windows was opaque for half their length, so it was impossible to see who was inside.

Linnet took a deep breath, pushed the door, and walked into a room which gave the impression that little had changed since the famous writer had patronised it back in the Thirties. The wood-panelled walls and partly frosted windows kept it pleasantly cool, and formal, white-jacketed waiters added to the air of bygone elegance. The clientele were all fashionably and expensively dressed, well-heeled Italians, with, judging from the hum of chatter, an admixture of Americans.

Max was seated at a corner table by a window, and he was not alone. A strikingly attractive young woman with long, shining black hair dressed in an immaculate French plait, and great, elongated eyes like amber lamps in her smoothly tanned face, was talking animatedly, telling him some long story, while he listened with that half-amused smile. Her hand, sparkling with rings, rested lightly on his sleeve, and he joined in her laughter at the conclusion of the tale.

'*Signorina*?' The waiter appeared discreetly at her elbow, and Linnet was aware that she must look gauche and unsure, hovering in the doorway. But she was reluctant to go over to Max's table while he was so obviously and pleasantly occupied. How many hours had he whiled away here, with women like this, when he was married to Joanna? she wondered, anger and distress flaring up inside her again.

'I——' She did not know what to say or do, but at that moment Max glanced up and spotted her. She saw him say something to the black-haired woman, who smiled, leaned over and gave him a brief kiss on the cheek, before drifting off to a group seated at another table.

He rose and came over to her, with a swift, fluid movement of long limbs, totally at ease and unhurried.

'How long have you been standing there? You should have come across,' he said, leading her back to the table.

'You appeared to be busy,' she said stiffly, perching on the edge of her chair.

'Oh, one always sees people one knows in here,' he said. 'It's a regular watering-hole.' He looked up at the waiter who was standing attentively at his side. '*Due aperitivo* "Harry", *per favore*,' he said, without troubling to ask Linnet what she would like.

'Do you always do that?' she demanded, suddenly feeling argumentative.

'Do what?' He looked down at her, surprised but untroubled.

'Order for people you don't know, with whose tastes you aren't familiar. Women do have minds of their own, you know. We aren't living in the Dark Ages!'

Linnet's grey eyes, usually cool, were sparkling angrily, and her pale skin was bright now with annoyance, not embarrassment. What did it matter if she let him have a piece of her mind? She wasn't going to work for him, therefore she was under no obligation to be diplomatic.

He was regarding her with an appreciative humour which only served to increase her irritation.

'You have quite a lot of spirit, for such a diminutive creature who looks as if a gust of wind might blow her away,' he said calmly. 'But take my advice and save all that fervour for a worthy cause. I merely ordered you a speciality of the house, which, as a native Venetian, I thought you might enjoy. It hardly merits banishing me to the Doge's dungeons.'

Linnet glowered at him, opened her mouth, shut it again, and bit her lip. She had jumped eagerly at a chance to take him down a peg, and instead he had put her firmly in her place. She hated him more than ever—his dry wit, his sleepy but observant blue eyes, the inbred, unquestioned autocracy of his demeanour—everything about him!

The drinks arrived, well chilled and ruby-coloured.

'Only sip. It's quite strong,' he advised patronisingly, as if she were a child at a party.

Linnet forced down her anger and managed a cool stare. She swallowed a mouthful experimentally and said, 'Gin and red vermouth, at a guess.'

His brows rose fractionally, and he inclined his head in brief agreement. 'Either you are very knowledgeable or you have a well-developed sense of taste.'

She gave a half-smile. 'If you really want to know, my parents own a country hotel. I'm no stranger at lending a hand behind the cocktail bar.'

'I see. And where might that be?'

'In Sussex.'

It had slipped out, quite inadvertently, in an unguarded moment. Not that it mattered now, but she realised how difficult it would have been to work for him and constantly watch her tongue. He was too sharp not to add up the associations if she scattered clues around so liberally in everyday conversation.

'My wife came from Sussex, but it's a part of England I don't know,' he said. 'I never visited it with her. Matters keep me mostly in mainland Europe.'

I'll bet they do, Linnet thought grimly. And he did not seem to mind alluding to them with barefaced unconcern.

'I haven't really lived there myself for some time. I was studying music in London,' she said, wondering how soon she could decently tell him of her decision, and escape. The longer she spent with him, the more he disconcerted her. One way or another, she knew she would remember this man for a long time. Dislike him fiercely she might—she *did*—but he had made an indelible impression on her. She had met no one remotely like him.

'Have you eaten?' he asked suddenly.

'Er—no,' she said, startled out of her darker thoughts by this mundane question.

'I assumed not. No one does here, that early. So I am going to risk ordering for you again, another delicacy of the house—*tagliolini verde gratinati*. Everyone likes pasta, so I should be reasonably safe from accusations of chauvinism of one sort or another.'

There was a hint of laughter lurking in his voice, and Linnet felt doubly uncomfortable.

'No, really... I can eat at the hotel...' she began, unhappy about his buying her a meal when she was about to turn down his offer. But that was silly...he was picking up the tab at the hotel, too. Maybe it was more that she felt oppressed and disturbed by his easy but all too palpable masculinity, and wanted only to get away from it.

But it was too late; he had already signalled the waiter, who wrote down the order and disappeared. Her escape route was blocked, at least for as long as it took for the food to be cooked and eaten. There was nothing she could do but endure her own growing uneasiness.

'Cosima has talked constantly of you since you left this afternoon,' he said. 'It is all, "When will Linnet come again?"'

Linnet swallowed guiltily.

'And what... what did you tell her?' she faltered.

'What do you think?' he countered. 'That I would bring you home gift-wrapped and tied with pink ribbon?'

Which did not answer her question, and was not intended to, she thought wryly. But however it was phrased she was sure she understood the gist of it. What Max di Angeli wanted he expected to get.

The waiter brought them green pasta with a sauce of chopped ham and cheese, and a carafe of chilled white Soave wine. It was simple and excellent, and Linnet could not pretend she did not enjoy it.

'Cosima is a child with a lot of affection to give, but she does not take instantly to everyone,' Max said soberly. 'I suggest you come to us for two weeks—as a guest—at the end of which time the choice to stay or not is still yours.'

'You are taking it for granted that I am going to come at all,' she retorted.

He shrugged.

'*Perché no*? You are, at the moment, a golden songbird without a song. But here in Italy you will live surrounded by music and beauty. Cosima, at the moment, has a need for someone like you. Perhaps you also have a need for her?'

He could not know what he was saying. It was not possible. Her affection for Cassie stemmed from the fact that she was Joanna's child, and unless he was a psychic he could not know that.

But it was true, none the less. If she walked away now, took the coward's route she had intended, she would break the fine thread of a bond stretching back into her childhood.

So instead of saying what she had meant to say to him Linnet heard herself replying quietly, 'Very well, *signore*. Two weeks.'

The golden songbird flies into the gilded cage, she thought ruefully, and still was not wholly sure why she had changed her mind and agreed to live under the same roof as this man whom she neither liked nor trusted.

For Cassie, of course, she told herself, for the sake of my friendship with her mother. But however she looked at it Maximiliano di Angeli had somehow persuaded her to do something all her basic instincts of self-preservation were screaming loudly against. For that reason alone, he was dangerous.

If Max had had his way entirely, Linnet would have been installed in the Ca' Favorita the next day. But, clinging on to her independence as fiercely as possible,

Linnet insisted she must go home for clothes and personal possessions.

'A waste of time,' he said impatiently.

'I came with an overnight bag,' she said firmly. 'I can't live out of that for a fortnight.'

'For this you are going to go back to England? Venice is full of shops, and I have accounts at all the best of them,' he said dismissively.

Let *him* provide her with a wardrobe? Absolutely not! She could well imagine the kind of expensive designer shops he would patronise.

'I couldn't do that,' she said quietly.

'Why?' he demanded. 'It would put you under no obligation, if that is what you are so afraid of. If money were the object here, I suppose your return air fare would be cheaper than a shopping spree, but it really isn't. Is it?'

'No. It isn't,' she agreed. 'I want my own things, *signore*. And I can pay my own air fare.'

'Rubbish.' He waved a scornful hand. 'And if you are going to live in my house... or only stay there as a guest... you are going to have to stop addressing me as *signore*. Would Max involve too great an effort?'

Linnet gulped.

'No, I suppose not,' she said grudgingly, although she feared the use of his name might stick in her throat. First names were for friends—or at least for people who had a reasonably amicable relationship. It was not the way you addressed a man for whom you nursed a deep, burning, hidden resentment. She was going to have to be a better actress than this to carry off such a deception for only a limited time.

He insisted on walking her the short distance back to the hotel, and before they left the bar she saw him wave to the black-haired woman he had been talking to when she'd arrived. He would be back here as soon as he was free of her, Linnet suspected. Perhaps they had already arranged to meet. Why she should feel guilty for keeping him from his obviously far more interesting private life she did not quite understand.

The light was beginning to fade as they walked, and Venice was enveloped in the golden afterglow of a splendid sunset.

'In this light, one can see why the city is known as "La Serenissima",' he mused. 'Venice is like an ageing but still beautiful courtesan, still sure of her worth, and her power to enchant.'

Linnet glanced sharply at him, and quickly looked away again, but his attention was on the floodlit splendour of the Salute, reflected in the darkening water. There was no doubt he loved his city, and felt in harmony with it. No doubt, also, that he cared for his daughter.

But... she sensed an easy, arrogant possessiveness behind his love for both... as if everything was his by right, by birth, and he never paused to question his ownership. His women would be subject to the same haughty, proprietorial assumptions, she felt sure. They would want for nothing materially, but they would be his possession.

She suppressed a shudder.

'Venice is very lovely,' she agreed, trying to deflect her mind from speculation about his personal life. Joanna had lived with this man; he had been her husband... her lover... In some distant, half-closed recess of her mind, she recalled being at Verne Hall one afternoon shortly before Joanna had flown off to Italy to get married, and hearing her giggling with some of her girlfriends.

'...and everyone knows that Italians make splendid lovers...' she was saying. Then, seeing that Linnet, who was much younger, was listening, 'Shush!'

Now, Linnet looked determinedly ahead of her, not wanting to wonder if it was true of the man at her side, not wanting even to *think* about such things in relation to him, although it was difficult not to, when she was almost certain he would soon be hurrying back to be with a beautiful woman. Her animosity towards him sharpened, complicated by something else which had no name she knew...a dark, unholy fascination she mentally stamped on as hard as she could, frantic to exterminate it.

So tangled was she in her own deep, guilty ruminations that she almost missed the practical arrangements he was outlining for her arrival at Ca' Favorita, and, horrified, she pulled herself up and listened attentively, sure that he would not be a man to forgive mistakes easily. His voice was matter-of-fact now, the voice of an employer talking calmly but authoritatively to one who took orders from him, and Linnet bristled inwardly at his tone. She had not, as yet, committed herself to that.

As they reached the entrance to her hotel, and she sensed him about to make a swift departure, she could not prevent herself from saying, 'One thing puzzles me...'

His faint, slightly impatient smile was touched with condescension. '*Mi dica*. Tell me.'

She paused, then rushed on. 'You offered me this position after a brief interview...principally because you say your daughter took a liking to me. But what if she had not met me...if I hadn't happened to come across her on the patio?'

His soft laugh was incredulous with mockery.

'You think that was an accident? How very naïve you must be,' he said bluntly.

Linnet's eyes widened angrily.

'You mean to tell me that was all a set-up... that you arranged to have Cassie out there with her skipping-rope every time you interviewed an applicant?'

The laughter was harsher now. 'Don't be ridiculous,' he said, with strained patience. 'Cosima is in her own home, and moves around it as freely as any child of her age. But yes, I ensured that each applicant happened to meet her.' His smile was so aloof as to be disdainful. 'I can make an accurate assessment in a very short time, I assure you,' he said, 'but I would not make this one without taking Cosima's feelings into account. How could I?'

While she was still staring at him, open-mouthed with the outraged awareness of having been manipulated—and without even realising it—he suddenly and quite unexpectedly took her hand in his.

'Have a safe journey,' he said. 'I expect you back in three days' time. *Arrivederci*.'

She stood in the doorway of the hotel, watching his tall figure stride quickly along the waterside *fondamente*. His handshake had been perfunctory and formal, but her fingers tingled with the powerful after-shock of his touch, as if he carried a live current of electricity. She could not say if she liked the sensation or not, which in itself was worrying.

She had come here predisposed to find him a heartless Casanova, a straightforwardly hedonistic and careless playboy, but the man she had met was more complex, more difficult to read than the simple stereotype she'd had in mind. Which did not make her detest him any the less, she assured herself ferociously. Haughty, imperious know-it-all—— A rogue impulse to run after him and, catching him unawares, push him into the Grand Canal shocked Linnet with its vigour.

But even if she succeeded, what would be the point? He was Max di Angeli, darling of the gods, and he would probably only come up smelling of roses!

Linnet's second arrival at the Ca' Favorita was considerably warmer than the first. The same manservant, Gianni, opened the door to her, but his manner was less forbidding, and he even managed a smile of recognition.

Immediately behind him came a slim, handsome woman in her fifties, with definite features and black hair swept up on top of her head in a 'cottage loaf' style. She wore a knitted skirt and jacket in soft pink, and beneath it a softly tailored ivory silk shirt with a delicate cameo brooch pinned at the neckline. Very Italian, down to her beautiful suede brogues, Linnet decided, glad to see that her smile was pleasantly welcoming.

'Come in, my dear girl. We speak English to begin, yes? I am Dina Freddi, and you, of course, are the girl with the name of a bird... how is it?'

'Linnet,' Linnet supplied. 'How do you do, Signora Freddi?'

'Do? How do I do what? Oh, I see!' She laughed, and her brown eyes danced very mischievously for a lady of her years. 'My English, she is not so good, no?'

Linnet liked her instantly.

'My Italian is far worse,' she admitted, but she could see now why this was not the English Max di Angeli wanted his daughter to fall into using, fluent and understandable though it might be. Dina Freddi was actually Max's widowed aunt, he had told her. She lived at the

Ca' Favorita, and hers was the authority on all domestic matters . . . and everything else, in his absence.

'We manage well enough, I think. Come and have some tea. You must be tired. Gianni, he see to your bags.'

She led Linnet not into the sumptuous drawing-room where she had been interviewed, but across a corridor into a much smaller, cosier room which appeared to be her particular sanctuary. There were comfy chairs that looked as if they had seen long service, a walnut bureau with household accounts spread out on it, and even a small fridge and an electric hob.

'Sometime I want tea, coffee, I not want to wait for someone else to make,' Dina Freddi said briskly, as the kettle started to sing. 'You like tea *al limone*?'

'Oh . . . *al latte*, please . . . with milk.'

'You learn quick, I think,' Dina said as she poured tea. 'We drink much tea together? Max, he never drinks tea, only coffee, coffee . . . I say, "No wonder you not stop, always busy, rushing about . . ."'

Sipping her tea, Linnet wondered if they were talking about the same person. Max di Angeli, of the lazily watchful blue eyes and relaxed, long-limbed body? She supposed frantic party-going and bar-lounging could take its toll after a while!

'It must have been a great shock for him, to lose his wife so young,' she said, aware that already she was fishing, but surely it was a reasonable comment for someone new in the household to make?

Dina's pursed lips and sudden stiffness of posture did not quite add up to the flood of Latin grief Linnet might have expected.

'*Si*, a shock, but not so much surprise. She always drive too fast, do everything too fast,' she said, on a note of disapproval.

Linnet bit on her astonishment. Venice, of course, was completely car-free, but she had seen enough around the airport to guess that the Italians merited their reputation as Europe's fastest, most insouciant drivers, so coming from one of them this was hard to stomach. She remembered Joanna whipping around the Sussex lanes in her maroon MG, and yes, she'd driven fast, but always superbly in control, as she had ridden. It had been Joanna's state of mind, not her ability at the wheel, which had caused her accident, in Linnet's opinion.

'Restless...' Dina muttered, shaking her head. 'Always restless... always she want to be somewhere else, never happy...'

Well, no, one wouldn't be happy if one were married to a dedicated womaniser, Linnet thought, with some annoyance. She wanted desperately to say something in defence of Joanna, her friend, who had come to this house as a bright and pretty young bride, but how could she, to Max's aunt? Especially since she was not supposed to know anything about those two and their marital difficulties.

Fortunately, just then they were interrupted by a scamper of footsteps in the corridor, the door burst open, and Cassie hurled herself into the room.

'Linnet, Linnet, Papà said you were coming! How long shall you stay?' she cried eagerly.

'Oh... a week or two, I guess,' she smiled. Max had been emphatic that Cassie's hopes must not be raised and then dashed; therefore she had no idea that Linnet was here other than as a friend on a visit. 'Perhaps we can go for some walks and boat rides around Venice? You will have to show me the way, since I'm new here.'

'Lovely!' Cassie squealed. Over the child's head, Linnet encountered Dina Freddi's sober gaze. There were questions she would have loved to ask, but dared not. Perhaps the worst of the grief and horror were behind her... a few months was a long time to a five-year-old... but Cassie hardly seemed like a little girl whose mother had died so recently. The centre of her world had collapsed, but she appeared happy and untroubled.

'We show Linnet her room now, Cassie,' Dina suggested, and Linnet followed the two of them, Cassie at a mad scramble, and Dina walking at a more stately pace, up a flight of stairs, along a corridor, up yet more stairs. Like most of the Venetian *palazzi*, the Ca' Favorita's frontage on its canal was imposing but fairly narrow; however, the house was deep, far larger than it appeared from outside, and the rooms towards the rear filled all manner of odd shapes and corners in the anatomy of the area. Linnet thought she would need a map to find her way around it.

Her room was one of those oddly shaped, tucked-away crannies, almost hexagonal, but quite charming. The bed was covered by a beautiful lace spread, which Dina told her had been hand-made by craftswomen on the island of Burano, in the Venetian lagoon; she had her own ornately tiled shower compartment, and her window looked out on a secretive little alley leading off between tall houses on either side.

'I told Papà you would like this room, so he said of course you must have it,' Cassie said solemnly.

'You were right—I like it very much, and I will say thank you to him,' Linnet promised, well aware that the decision had been made more to gratify his daughter than to please her.

'Oh, you can't do that—he isn't here,' Cassie said casually, kneeling on the deep window-sill to watch pigeons alighting on the roof-tops opposite.

Linnet glanced at Dina with a question in her eyes, and the older woman nodded.

'Is true. Max is away—in Geneva,' she confirmed.

'When will he be back?' Linnet asked. She had expected this man, who had all but ordered her to spend time in his house, to be here to greet her, at least. But no—having made the arrangements to suit him, he had cheerfully gone off about his own affairs, whatever they were.

Dina shrugged. 'Perhaps one week, perhaps more. It depends,' she said. 'He will phone to tell me when he will return.'

Meanwhile the child was left here, with Dina—who, it had to be said, clearly loved her very much—and a houseful of servants. What way was that to treat a motherless little girl? What was he doing in Geneva that was so vital that his daughter, who needed him more than ever now, was deprived of a father, too? It was too late for skiing, so he must be someone's house guest. Or maybe it was yet another woman?

Linnet turned away, sickened, to hide the disgusted curling of her lip. Children needed more than absent, caring concern, however sincere. They needed a parent who was actively *there*. Sooner or later, even though it might not be diplomatic, might even be downright foolhardy, Linnet knew she would be unable to prevent herself from telling Max di Angeli this!

Much to her own surprise, she settled in very easily at the Ca' Favorita. In spite of the grandeur of its formal rooms, and the obvious wealth displayed in their furnishings and works of art, there was an almost informal atmosphere about the *palazzo*. Dina Freddi had a firm but friendly hand on the reins of its management, with

Signora Marchetti, the housekeeper, directly responsible to her. Then there was Gianni, who seemed to do just about everything around the place, Aldo, the temperamental but highly talented chef, and two cheerful maids who kept the *palazzo* spick and span.

Twice a week, the music teacher, who was a genial and bespectacled elderly man, came to give Cassie her piano lessons, which she loved, and she attended a regular dancing class. Dina asked Linnet if she would mind taking Cassie to these, and she agreed readily, since it gave her the chance to explore Venice while the child was practising her *pliés* and arabesques.

The city had seduced her swiftly. She was completely captivated and loved to walk its narrow streets, crossing the bridges over the canals, gazing at all she saw, equally enraptured by ancient buildings and everyday scenes.

Her second week was drawing to a close as she walked one morning with Cassie from the *sestriere* of San Polo, the district in which the Ca' Favorita was situated, and after leaving her at dancing class carried on towards the Rialto bridge. Here, the Grand Canal was wide, majestic, and always busy, and she loved to stand at the mid-point of the bridge, gazing at the vista before her, ever-changing, yet somehow a scene that had endured for more than five hundred years.

Only too aware that her allotted trial period was almost up, she was surprised at the sudden darkening of her spirits at the thought of leaving this unique place . . . not only that, but never seeing Cassie again, of whom she had quickly grown so fond, never again drinking tea in Dina's room, or stepping from the water-gate into the cool beauty of the Ca' Favorita.

And Max? What about him? Linnet looked down pensively into the sunlit water of the canal. She had seen nothing of him since her arrival, but surely she would, since it was to him that she must give her decision. Every day she had wondered if he would turn up, although Dina had said nothing, and the thought of meeting once again that nonchalant blue stare, hearing the voice full of velvet scorn, quickened her pulse with apprehension . . . and a guilty excitement she struggled to suppress. She exhaled deeply, impaled on the horns of a dilemma, unable to decide which would be harder—to stay or to leave.

'This is not the Bridge of Sighs, you know. You're in the wrong spot altogether.'

She jumped. The voice spoke almost in her ear, and so closely followed the path of her imagination that she thought for a brief second that it was a figment of it. But no . . . it was Max di Angeli himself, and, turning, she confronted the lithe reality of his body, close to hers among a sudden press of people crossing the bridge, so near that she could feel its warmth, and could not escape without making a great performance of it.

He was more casually dressed today, the summer-weight trousers, fine leather belt and soft, short-sleeved taupe-coloured shirt in a silky material all of a quiet, understated elegance that spoke more surely of quality than any amount of flamboyance could have done.

She looked up into his face, closer than she had ever seen it, struck by the fine texture of his lightly tanned skin, the curve of his mouth, only half-smiling, the healthy gleam of the black hair winging back from his brow. The gentian eyes were partly veiled as he regarded her steadily from beneath lowered lids.

Her breath caught hard in her throat, and there was a sharp, inexplicable pain just beneath her ribs. For an unguarded moment she forgot who he was, forgot all that she knew about him. There was no hatred or suspicion, because there was no past, no history, no Joanna, only herself, standing here on a bridge in Venice, with the most devastating and intriguing man a girl could hope to meet, in her wildest dreams. The sunlight danced on the water, pigeons wheeled in the blue sky, and the poignant romance of the ancient city wrapped itself sinuously around them.

'So—Linnet,' he said softly, questioningly, resting one hand either side of her on the worn parapet of the bridge, and easing in to allow two plump, black-clad nuns and a group of Japanese tourists to pass. The contact of his body all along the length of hers shocked her with the force of its physical reality. The maleness of him, lean and hard, left her all the more conscious of her own pliant femininity. She felt helpless and vulnerable, and yet, beneath it, the fierce springs of a woman's strength of emotion she had not yet tested surged and bubbled.

'What a crowd—it's a sign summer is coming,' he murmured prosaically. 'Let's get out of here—we're blocking the traffic.'

She stiffened as he put a directing hand under her elbow to steer her across the bridge, but she looked straight ahead, avoiding his eyes, frantic to ensure he gleaned nothing of the turmoil inside her, the foolishness of her emotions.

It was quite obvious that the proximity of her body had not moved or excited him in the least, and indeed why should it? He must be sated with beautiful, glamorous women.

What had he called her, the last time they met—a diminutive creature? She didn't interest him, and how could she allow herself, even for a fleeting moment, to feel attracted by a man of his sort? It had been nothing but a brief fantasy, a mirage induced by the seductive atmosphere of Venice.

Maybe if she kept on telling herself this as firmly as possible she would eventually believe it. She had to. The alternative was quite unthinkable!

CHAPTER THREE

MAX insisted on buying coffee, and they sat at a waterside café overlooking the Rialto, protected from the sun by bright red canvas awnings.

'I didn't know you were coming back today,' Linnet said. 'Signora Freddi didn't tell me you'd phoned.'

'Nor had I, although I usually do, but I had a brief gap in my schedule, and there was a flight available. Aunt Dina told me you had taken Cosima to dancing class, so I thought I might find you somewhere around here.'

Linnet tried not to think about his schedule, or the gaps in it, as she tried equally hard not to relive those few moments on the Rialto bridge, when she had felt the breath being squeezed out of her body by unseen forces. It had been a trick of the imagination, no more, she told herself firmly.

'You do seem to travel around Europe quite a lot,' she observed, unable to keep the slight note of censure from her voice.

His smile was cool. 'Naturally. I'm a pan-European in every sense of the word, as are most families like mine. Our family tree has branches as far apart as Spain and Austria. I was educated in France and Germany, in addition to a spell in England. Try not to be provincial, Linnet. The pond is wider than you think.'

She gasped with indignation.

'Provincial—me?' she exploded. 'I was about to study in Italy myself, and what could be more international than the world of music?'

'Then you should understand my background a little,' he said imperturbably. 'Finish your coffee, and we'll go and collect Cosima.'

Linnet could have pointed out that studying or working abroad was one thing—flitting about socially was quite another. Where had Max been when Joanna was hiding her broken heart at Verne Hall? 'Oh, he's skiing at Val d'Isere, or St Moritz, or if the snow's finished there no doubt he'll take himself and his party off to Aspen, Colorado,' Joanna had said sourly. 'You have to move fast to keep up with Max.'

But how much was it politic to reveal she knew about his social life, after so brief an acquaintance? She said only, 'I understand that Cassie misses you when you are not here!'

He frowned down at her.

'And I her. But it would be quite unsuitable for her to travel around with me, as I'm sure you must appreciate.'

'I'm sure it would,' she said quite tartly, cheeks burning. There were aspects of her father's life to which it would be quite wrong for Cassie to be exposed, and Linnet was only amazed that he did not object to admitting this openly.

A faint puzzlement showed in his lifted brow, and the aloof curl of his upper lip. 'What is it, I wonder, that you are trying, very circuitously and without much success, to say?' he asked coldly.

Linnet gulped. What *was* she trying to say? Get out of the fast lane, put your libido on hold, and be a parent? Not even if she was going to turn and walk away immediately afterwards, and never see him again, could she have broached this subject to Max di Angeli, who had stopped in his tracks and was looking at her with such hauteur, and a glint of danger in the no longer amused blue eyes. He would tell her to mind her own damn business, that how he lived his life was entirely up to him, and she would probably die of embarrassment on the spot.

'That it would be better if you could spend more time here in Venice,' she suggested daringly, waiting for the avalanche of his anger to fall on her head.

However, he merely shrugged.

'That's not possible,' was all he said, very clearly and finally, and set off walking again at a brisk pace, so that Linnet had to run to catch up with him. His tone indicated that the subject was closed, and it was perhaps just as well that they had reached the dancing school just as the pupils were spilling out.

'Papà!' Cassie hurled herself ecstatically into her father's arms, and after hugging him thoroughly said with almost adult reproachfulness, 'It was very naughty of you to ask Linnet to stay, and then to go away.'

'But I knew you and Aunty Dina would look after her, *piccola*,' he said.

'Oh, we did. We've had a nice time,' Cassie insisted, trotting along between the two of them. 'Lots of walks and boat rides, and Linnet brought some lovely books from England.'

'Books?'

He glanced questioningly at Linnet over Cassie's head, and she said nervously, 'They're just some old children's books of mine. I thought Cassie might like them. *Winnie-the-Pooh*, and that sort of thing.'

For a moment she hovered under the weight of his anticipated disapproval. Then he said, 'Very well, but I would prefer it if you had asked me—or, in my absence, Signora Freddi—about reading material, first.'

It was a rebuke, however calmly delivered, and Linnet knew her face was pink again. The books had been a last-minute thought, but she had been glad of them when she had observed the dearth of children's literature in English at the Ca' Favorita.

'Cassie doesn't have many English books,' she remarked defensively.

'No?' A slight frown furrowed his brow, and she thought she picked up a faint note of derision as he said, 'I might have realised that. My wife was not much of a reader herself, beyond glossy fashion magazines. We shall have to remedy the lack.'

He was talking as if her decision to stay had already been given, taking it for granted, and she supposed it never occurred to him that the rest of the world would do other than fall in with his wishes. In theory, she could still choose to leave, but Linnet felt her freedom of will and action draining away from her. Her growing attachment to Cassie, the spell of Venice and the Ca' Favorita were enmeshing her like trap-nets—as he had known they would, damn him!

That night, after Cassie was in bed, she had dinner with Max and Dina in the formal dining-room whose tall windows overlooked the canal. Outside, lamplight and the glow from lighted windows refracted wavily in the silken water. Within, there was the gleam of polished wood beneath ornate silver candelabra, the brittle sparkle of fine Venetian glassware that looked too precious to use, the shine of solid silver cutlery.

Max was resplendent in a dark blue velvet jacket, tailored with casual perfection, the cuffs of his white lawn shirt barely showing at the wrists. The many strands of his ancestry were perfectly meshed. The eyes were perhaps inherited from some Austrian forebear, while the prototype of that long-limbed body might have fought with Charlemagne. But the unmistakably sensual curl of his lips, the eloquently speaking hands were pure Latin.

She could not help studying him, covertly, she hoped, as he poured pre-dinner *aperitivos*, but some extra sense must have alerted him to her cautiously appraising scrutiny.

'You look very charming, too,' he said, with an infuriatingly confident grin.

Linnet teetered between anger and embarrassment. That he should assume she was gazing at him in admiration was the most infernal conceit, implying that no woman could resist him. To acknowledge her supposed admiration aloud was unfair, and could only have been deliberately calculated to discomfit her.

'I was just thinking that you would not look out of place in the party scene from "*La Traviata*",' she said, quite forgetting that whenever she tried to put one over on him he always succeeded in making it rebound on her.

He laughed lightly. 'But you would need a bustle and a few more years on your back to play Violetta,' he said. 'Doesn't the plot concern a young man captivated by an experienced older woman? I see you more as Mimi in "*La Bohème*"—young, innocent and alone in a wicked city.'

Linnet's fingers curled into her palms as she struggled with a desire for vengeance she could not satisfactorily express.

'I am neither as green nor as defenceless as you seem to think!' she exclaimed in a low, furious voice.

'No, I'm sure you have sharp claws, songbird,' he said silkily. 'I was speaking of appearances only. And, as I already told you, yours is particularly attractive tonight.'

He had turned the tables on her twice in as many minutes, with virtually the same breath telling her that he considered her naïve, then paying her a compliment. Was it the skilful use of such unnerving tactics which brought women to his feet, as Joanna had hinted? But why waste them on *her*? Or couldn't he help it—was it something he did unthinkingly, so automatically that it was almost a reflex?

'Do I hear you two talking of the opera?' Dina enquired lightly, drifting over from the door, where she had been conferring with Gianni over some matter. Dina was an enthusiast, Linnet knew. The two of them had had several interesting discussions on the subject over the last week or two. 'Please do tell us, Linnet—which is the operatic heroine you would most like to play?'

A demon of mischief caught Linnet in its grasp, a refusal to be stereotyped, and she risked a sidelong glance at Max from beneath lowered eyelashes.

'Carmen,' she murmured demurely.

His gaze remained on her, steady and speculative. Laughter lurked in its depths, but to give him his due he did not give way to it. He simply looked at Linnet, slim and ethereal in her silky, apple-green dress, her pale gold hair caught up on top of her head, the candle-glow flattering her translucent English skin and cool, opal-grey eyes.

'Carmen,' he echoed, the single word conjuring up the passionate, superstitious, black-haired gypsy girl who drove men wild, and was killed by an ex-lover in a jealous rage. 'In my opinion, that would be a highly original casting.'

'You may think so, but appearances can be deceptive. You have never heard me sing,' she pointed out quietly.

The humour in his eyes faded, to be replaced by something she could have sworn was regret, and again she felt that painful constriction of her breath.

'More is the pity,' he said soberly. 'But maybe I shall have that pleasure, one day.'

It was Dina who unconsciously defused the moment, which had become so heavy with meaning for Linnet that it was almost unbearable.

'*Si*, when Linnet is very famous, Max, we shall be proud to say she was a guest in our house,' she said brightly. 'But for now dinner is ready—shall we go to the table?'

Linnet found it impossible to sit and eat and not be aware all the time of Max. She could scarcely concentrate on the excellent *zuppa di pesce* they ate as a first course, obviously freshly made from the amazing variety of fish she had seen slithering and shining on the stalls at the morning market on the Rialto.

He sat at the head of the table, with Dina at his right hand and Linnet on his left, and talked easily, casually, as he took over from Gianni the task of refilling their wine glasses. He was playing the perfect host, she saw, talking about his city and all that was to be seen in and around it, conversation designed to interest the stranger and put her at her ease. That Linnet remained uncomfortable was no fault of his impeccable manner, but a direct result of his inescapable charisma, and the ever-increasing effect it was having on her.

She tried to eat, for the food at the Ca' Favorita was always excellent, and she had done it full justice during her stay. There was pork, delicately fennel-flavoured and cooked in milk, there were stuffed, baked peaches, cheese, and a bowl of ripe, fresh fruit, all of it perfect.

'Not hungry today?' Dina asked worriedly, observing Linnet's lack of appetite.

'I'm sorry—I think I overdid the ice-cream in the *gelateria* this afternoon,' she excused herself swiftly, avoiding Max's quizzical glance, but unable to escape the certainty that he did not believe this explanation. She was quick to interpret the look that flashed between him and his aunt at the end of the meal, after which Dina rose, saying,

'I must write some letters, so I say *buona notte* to both of you, and I take coffee in my room.'

It was quite obviously a deliberate ploy to leave her and Max alone, and a shiver ran along Linnet's nerves. She found it was infinitely easier when the full force of his powerful personality was not directed solely at her. Without the shield of a third party, she felt so exposed and defenceless that she could almost have begged Gianni not to disappear after serving coffee, but the man-servant was far too well trained and discreet to remain where his presence was not required.

Max stood up, walked over to the long windows and opened them up, letting in the warm night, and a flood of moonlight. The cry of a passing gondolier, the splash of an oar stole in, evocatively, on the air, as he turned back towards her, tall and demanding, the glow from the candles casting odd planes of shadow across his face.

Linnet sat perfectly still, like an antelope watching a prowling tiger, unwilling to risk drawing the predator's attention by making the slightest move.

'Well, Linnet,' he said, the soft drawl of her name setting all her senses jangling afresh. 'How have you enjoyed your two weeks at the Ca' Favorita?'

She swallowed hard.

'Very much,' she answered truthfully. 'Everyone has been very kind, and it would be impossible not to adore Cassie.'

'A feeling which is clearly mutual,' he said drily. 'So—are you ready now to sign the contract?'

There was a world of confident certainty in his voice, and Linnet wondered if it had ever crossed his mind that she might say no. Cassie liked her, it suited him that she should stay, and that was that. Looking up at him, she was once again overcome by that sensation of powerlessness, of being somehow a captive, that she recalled from her very first visit to this house. She had not felt it since, and knew now that it was not the house at all—it was *him*. His was the force that troubled and unnerved her.

'I...I don't know...' she began.

'I think you do,' he said calmly, and with quiet emphasis. 'I've seen you with Cosima. I've seen how Venice has gripped your imagination. You'll stay, Linnet. Be in my study at nine tomorrow, ready to sign. Gianni will show you where it is. For now—have some more coffee.'

Linnet could only stare at him, mesmerised and unable to protest, because she knew he was right. She would indeed stay.

But the reasons he had so plainly stated, true though they were, were only half the story. How could she walk out of the Ca' Favorita, when she was in the grip of so powerful a fascination—a fascination of which he was the object?

Joanna had come here, seven years earlier, because she was in love with this man, and, although it would be unfair to say he had killed her, indirectly she was dead because of him.

Linnet knew this, and although she had tried and condemned Max di Angeli in her mind her disobedient senses were still enthralled by him.

Lying in bed that night, listening to the mysterious waterborne sounds that never quite ceased, hearing the church clocks strike every hour, she found it hard to say who she despised the most—him, or herself.

In the morning, of course, things looked brighter, as they always did. Linnet was up, dressed and had a firm grip on herself by the time she was due to keep her appointment at Max's study. She had almost, if not quite, convinced herself that she was indeed staying purely because of her affection for Cassie and her desire to see more of Venice, and that Max himself had little to do with her decision. By his own admission, and from what she had already observed, he was rarely here, so she would see little of him.

All the same, her heart was skipping to an irregular beat as she followed Gianni along the labyrinthine inner corridors of the *palazzo* to a room tucked away at the rear, which she never would have found for herself. Her throat was tight, and her palms sticky, as Gianni tapped on the door and opened it for her to enter, and she had the strong sensation of taking a momentous and irrevocable step.

Her head high, her eyes ready to meet those of Max di Angeli without flinching, she all but gasped in astonishment to find that he was not present at all. There was only Dina, smiling as usual, and a dry, efficient-looking man seated behind the large mahogany desk, with papers spread out before him.

He was introduced to her as Signor Rinaldi, the di Angeli family lawyer, and in slow, careful English he explained to her that he had the power of attorney to sign on behalf of his client, and showed her where she herself should sign.

Linnet's puzzled gaze flew to Dina. 'Max will not be here?' she asked.

'No, he went very early this morning, to Rome,' Dina told her. 'But not to worry—no problem. You sign, yes?'

Almost in a daze, Linnet appended her signature to the paper, hardly listening as the lawyer explained to her that she was committing herself to employment for a period of not less than six months. Why did she have this awful feeling of signing away her freedom, her will, her independence? Six months was hardly a life sentence. And what difference did it make that Max was not present to witness her doing so?

Perhaps at the root of her unease was the fact that he had chosen not to tell her last night that he would not be here in person. He must have known, but he had consciously deceived her. It came back to her anew, with great force, that this was not a man she could trust. He followed his own rules, and ignored those the rest of the world lived by. Joanna had discovered that too late, and as Linnet made her way back to the dining room for breakfast she told herself soberly, many times over, that she must never, ever forget it.

In effect, nothing changed with the signing of the contract, and Linnet's life at the Ca' Favorita went on much as before. She took Cassie out and about, read and chatted to her, and shared with Dina the duties involved in caring for the child. Since she enjoyed being with Cassie, life was not onerous, and she had plenty of free time in which to wander around Venice.

Living as she did in the *palazzo*, with a very luxurious roof over her head, and marvellous food set in front of her at every meal, Linnet hardly needed much in the way of money. As a music student on a fairly meagre grant, she had become used to a frugal existence. Money and its trappings had never really interested her, and it was not the motivating force which had brought her to Italy anyhow.

She had scarcely glanced at the paragraph on the contract which concerned her salary, so preoccupied had she been with her own emotional state at the time, and not until she read her own copy through, later, did it really dawn on her that Max was paying her what seemed to her a staggering sum simply to lead a pleasant and not overtaxing life.

'This cannot be right,' she had ventured to say tentatively to Dina. 'So much money—I really don't need or deserve to be so highly paid.'

Dina had merely shrugged.

'Accounts of house I do—nothing else,' she had said, disclaiming liability. 'No money is too much to Max, for Cassie. And you have...how you say?...responsibility.'

But she didn't, not really—short of seeing that her small charge did not fall into a canal, or stuff herself too full of ice-creams, and Linnet felt strongly that she was earning too much for doing too little. She resolved to speak to Max about it when he came back, which, according to Dina, would be in two days' time.

'He very busy. *Always*, always very busy,' she said, sighing a little, but there was pride in her voice, not criticism. Linnet wondered how a sensible woman like Dina could approve of her nephew's frenzied, peripatetic lifestyle, but it was hardly a subject she felt able to discuss with her. Perhaps Italian women of her class expected their menfolk to flit around Europe enjoying life to the full, distributing their favours as it suited them? It was all beyond Linnet's comprehension.

She knew when Max was back, the moment she walked into the house. Cassie had her music lesson that morning, and Linnet had been over to Dorsoduro to look at the Guggenheim collection of twentieth-century art. Fast becoming a practised traveller around Venice, she had hopped on a *vaporetto* at the Accademia bridge, and sat enjoying the breeze which tempered heat that was growing steadily as May moved into June. She walked from the Rialto, along the little back alleys she had discovered which brought her to the *palazzo's* rear entrance, and thence into the patio, and in those few minutes along the corridor she became aware of a greater bustling in the service quarters, an air of purpose and urgency. Indeed, Aldo almost bumped into Linnet as she passed the door to the kitchens.

'*Scusi*, Signorina Linnet! Signor Max is home,' he said, hurrying about his business, doubtless revising the dinner menu in his head as he did so. Max was 'Signor Max' to all the servants, part of the informality of this household which rescued it from too much grandeur.

Gianni, whom she encountered crossing the patio, informed her, when she asked, that the *signore* was in his study, and Linnet took her courage in both hands and decided to confront him there and then about the matter of her salary. It never helped to put off anything one was afraid to do, and facing Max di Angeli fell well inside that category. Besides, who knew when he would be off on his travels again?

Her heart was in her mouth as she found her way to his study, and she stood outside the door for a full minute, plucking up the nerve to knock on it. This was ridiculous, she knew. He couldn't eat her! Lifting her hand, she rapped a little more loudly than she had intended, and the voice which told her to enter was fairly sharp, as if its owner did not wish to be disturbed and resented the brusque intrusion.

He was seated behind his desk, which was strewn with papers and empty coffee-cups, and his appearance gave Linnet a momentary shock. He looked tired—jaded, she thought, his eyes deep-set and heavy, his jaw dark with stubble, and instead of the crisp shirt and tie he sported a crew-necked sweatshirt that was slightly rumpled.

She hesitated, more unsure of herself before this tired, somewhat dishevelled stranger than she had felt when she was at the mercy of the immaculate individual he normally presented to the world.

'Ah—Linnet.' His voice was dry, distant.

'I... I wanted to have a word with you,' she all but whispered.

'Is it vital? I have had time neither to change nor shave, as you can see.' He ran a hand along his firm jawline, and winced with distaste.

'Well, no... yes... that is, it won't take a minute...' she floundered.

He sighed wearily. 'Oh, please do get on with it, Linnet, since you are here, if you are sure it isn't some simple problem that Aunt Dina could sort out,' he said impatiently.

'No. She can't—it isn't,' Linnet said, more firmly. 'It concerns my salary.'

A flicker of amusement crept into the tired blue eyes.

'You're asking for an increase—already?' he hinted. '*Dio mio*! I didn't think inflation was that bad!'

'It's hardly a matter for jest, and of course I wasn't asking for a raise,' Linnet retorted acidly. 'Quite the opposite, actually. I think you're paying me far too much for what I do. It's not necessary, especially since, living here, I hardly need to spend anything.'

He raised both hands in an eloquent gesture, as if he could hardly believe what he was hearing.

'Then spend, Linnet,' he said with a touch of exasperation. 'You are an unusual woman if you don't like shopping. We make beautiful leather goods here—shoes and bags. Jewellery and glassware are good, too. Or if you don't want to buy things put the money in the bank, for a rainy day. You have plenty of those in England, no? But don't complain to me, for heaven's sake. I pay you what I think the job is worth, and since you are looking after *my* daughter that is quite a lot. Don't ask me to undervalue her.'

Linnet was stung by his brisk, intolerant dismissal of her perfectly reasonable objections, but she was angered even more by something deeper—his airy assumption that distributing financial largesse, like some medieval merchant prince, was the answer to everything, the solution to all problems.

'There's more to life and to human relationships than simply money, Max!' she flashed, not realising until she had spoken that she had, in anger, used his name naturally for the first time. 'You can't put a price on Cassie, or on my care of her, or on your love for her, come to that. These things aren't valued in such terms!'

He looked hard at her.

'I have had the distinct feeling, on more than one occasion, that there is some point you are trying to make,' he said levelly. 'If that is the case, why don't you get on with it, instead of dropping heavy hints which serve no purpose?'

The very quietness of his voice sent warning messages shuddering down her spine. But she had backed away from this crisis before, and if she did so again would cease to respect herself, so she consigned her soul to whatever powers watched over it, and bit the bullet.

'The point is that Cassie needs you around more than any amount of money spent on her welfare,' she said, unable completely to suppress a suspicion of a tremor in her voice. 'The point is, surely, that parenthood should come before . . . before pleasure.'

'Pleasure, huh?' he said thoughtfully, picking up the last word quickly, where she had hesitated on it. 'You think I have just now returned from a pleasure jaunt—yes?'

The implications of the word hovered in the room all around them, and Linnet knew that without a doubt the meaning in both of their minds was identical. Pleasure—sex. Some woman's bed, where he had been amusing himself making love, to return in this exhausted, obviously debauched condition. If there had been any way she could have run from the room now, Linnet would have done so gladly, but his eyes, no longer dazed, were fastened firmly on her, and as she stood, transfixed, he rose slowly from his chair, towering over her across the desk.

'Well . . . and haven't you?' she countered defiantly.

'And if I have?' He threw the question back at her, his tone ominously soft. 'I'm a man—in my prime, wouldn't you say? Don't you think I am entitled to my . . . pleasures?' Again, he stressed the word deliberately, and suddenly Linnet knew he was positively enjoying subjecting her to this mortification. Max di Angeli had woken up, and was having fun—at her expense.

'That's not what I meant——' she began, floundering helplessly in the morass of her own making.

'No?' He eased himself from the space between desk and chair, and came round the desk towards her, perching lightly on the edge of it, so that his eyes were on a level with hers. 'Perhaps you intended to suggest I should save time and energy by keeping a woman under my roof, huh? A mistress, I think, is the rather old-fashioned word for it. Well, yes, I can see there would be certain advantages to such an arrangement.'

'This is crazy!' she said, with a sharpness born of fierce apprehension. 'I was trying to have a sensible discussion, and you are simply being facetious!'

'Not at all,' he smiled, shaking his head gently. 'I am impressed by your suggestion. It shows great initiative, and leads me to wonder if you were thinking of applying personally for the position. You would need to audition, naturally, but there's no time like the present...'

Linnet's gasp of outrage was pre-empted by the lightning speed of his movement. In the space of a heartbeat, he had uncoiled to his full length, his arm was around her waist, one hand firm and square as a vice in the small of her back, while the other cupped her head, right where it joined the slim column of her neck, forcing it back, fingers twisting painfully in the thick, soft locks of her hair. She could not struggle—the desk, behind her, ground into her hips, and his long, hard body pinioned her to it. She opened her mouth to cry out, but in the same instant it was stopped by his, full on it, the pressure almost bruising as he kissed her.

Linnet had never been kissed quite like this before—so forcefully, almost brutally, and totally without her consent. She had never been held so that she could not escape if she wanted to, had never felt herself so utterly and dangerously at a man's mercy as she did now.

So why wasn't she hating it, choking with revulsion, squirming with horror at the harsh treatment of his hands and his mouth? Why, instead, was she limp with response, her body not tense with resistance, but folding pliantly into his, her lips parting receptively and then—worse, far worse—giving back his kiss with a hungry eagerness she had never encountered or suspected in herself?

His hand moved down her back to her hips, moulding her more firmly to him, and with a shock she felt unmistakably that this man, far from being exhausted, was now fully awake and aroused and capable of anything... here, now, this minute! An intense shudder ran the length of her body from head to toe, and she shook, literally, as if she would explode into a thousand shattered fragments with the pressure building up inside her.

He let her go then, abruptly, and with a deep sense of shame she knew that she had surprised him with the strength of her response. He had not expected this fragile-looking English girl to be capable of such passion, any more than she had herself.

'Well,' he said, with quiet amazement. '*Va bene*. Don't call me, as they say, I'll call you!'

The taunt in his voice, the mocking laughter creeping back into his eyes hit Linnet like a bucket of iced water flung in her face. Funny, was it? Amused, was he, to find that she had a woman's feelings? He knew that now, all too well, and there was no way she could remain in this house with him, after such an exhibition.

'Don't bother!' she gasped out furiously. 'I won't be here—you can be very sure of that!'

The study door slammed behind her so hard that its echo followed her as she ran, sobbing with shame and fury, down the corridors of the *palazzo*, with only one thought in mind: to leave—to get away from here, away from him, right now, before her treacherous senses led her ever deeper into a maze of desire from which, she feared, there would be no escape.

CHAPTER FOUR

LINNET did not get very far in her headlong flight. Finding her way to Max's study in a state of relative calm and full possession of her senses had been one thing. Retreating in shattered disarray, her heart still thumping wildly from those dreadful, marvellous, shameful moments in his arms was something else, and the Byzantine layout of the *palazzo's* interior defeated her.

She came to an abrupt halt at a branch in the corridor. Should she turn right or left here? Somewhere, there was a flight of stairs, she was sure, but where? Linnet pressed a trembling hand to her forehead and found it damp with the perspiration of emotion. She was still well and truly a prisoner here, if she could not find her way out, or even back to the refuge of her own room.

'Lost, are you?'

She turned to find him standing in front of her, blocking her way, arms folded, the smile on his handsome face grim and not remotely reassuring.

'I want to go back to my room,' she stated, with as much dignity as she could summon up, and then, as he made no move, she could not resist adding nastily, 'You should provide visitors with a map and compass, or is it intentional that once they are allowed in they are never seen again?'

His smile deepened fractionally, but there was still no humour, and not a drop of sympathy in it.

'Put it down to the likelihood that fourteenth-century builders all had Machiavellian minds,' he suggested coolly. 'Meanwhile, I should go straight to lunch, if I were you. Come along—I'll point you in the right direction.'

He put a hand lightly under her elbow to turn her round, and she jumped back, flinching.

'Keep your hands off me!'

'Is *that* what you want me to do?' His frown was heavy with feigned surprise. 'You do amaze me, Linnet! I could have sworn that you . . . well, never mind.'

It was hard to look directly into the mocking blue eyes, but she forced herself to do it.

'*You* may take it for granted that women find you irresistible, but *I*, for one, do not go around looking for sexual harassment!' she snapped icily. 'You misunderstood me—misinterpreted me—quite deliberately, back there, and you know it!'

'Did I?' The smile was now a faint sleepy grin, with a suggestive hint at the corners. 'Well, you did rather ask for it, didn't you? Sat up and begged for it, in fact, taking it upon yourself to read me the riot act about matters that are none of your concern.' Beneath the silken drawl rasped an obbligato of steely censure. 'However, we'll say no more about it. This way, Linnet——'

He was ushering her along the corridor, and she was compelled to move quickly ahead of him for fear he might take hold of her again. She could not bear him to know how strongly his touch affected her.

Suddenly and unexpectedly they were on the patio.

'See, it's easy once you grasp the principle,' he said. 'This is the central point, and the corridors radiate from it. I'm sure you can find the dining-room from here. I must go and make myself presentable before I put in an appearance.'

She pulled up sharp and stared at him in utter disbelief. Hadn't he heard or understood a word she had said to him in his study? Or did he simply ignore what it did not suit him to hear?

'I do not want any lunch,' she said coldly and clearly. 'What I want—what I intend—is to pack my bags and get out of here, forthwith.'

His face was drawn into harder lines than she had ever seen on it, taut, determined and totally implacable.

'That is out of the question,' he said bluntly. 'You signed a contract, or have you already conveniently forgotten that? Your signature on a legal document is your word, Linnet. That may mean nothing to you, but I shall hold you to it, none the less.'

He had to be bluffing... didn't he? After all that had happened in the study, after what he had done, and the acrimony which had followed, for him to expect her to remain here as if it were all irrelevant was beyond the bounds of belief.

'You wouldn't do that...' she faltered, her nerve beginning to break.

'Try me,' he invited, his expression unchanged. 'Breach of contract is a serious matter, you know. You will need good lawyers, and they don't come cheap. Are you rich, Linnet, or are your parents? I am—and my lawyers will take you to the cleaners. This I promise.'

She saw that he was serious. There was no jesting quality underlying his tone now, and only a deadly certainty of purpose in his eyes. He was well aware she did not have enough money to challenge him in court, and he must know she would never expect her parents to put themselves in debt to help her to do so. She was trapped, and, her gaze flickering wildly around and coming back to rest helplessly on him, she said in a voice low with defeat, 'Why are you doing this to me? Why are you making me stay here against my will? You are rich enough, as you have just pointed out, to employ anyone you choose. Let me go!'

'I can't, and will not. And there's your reason why,' he said firmly but softly, and her gaze followed his to where Cassie, in pursuit of a fluffy white kitten, had trotted on to the patio. 'You disappoint me, Linnet. I would have thought affection for her alone would hold you, but since it won't I have to treat you simply as another employee, and insist you abide by the conditions of your employment.'

They both fell silent as Cassie came towards them, her face wreathed in smiles, the kitten squirming in her arms.

'Papà! Linnet! Look—isn't she beautiful?'

Linnet sobered, as just for a moment a pang of guilt shot through her. She still believed she had been entirely in the right to say what she had said to Max about his lifestyle, presumptuous as it might be considered. And, right or wrong, it had certainly not entitled him to treat her as he had—as if she were indeed a woman whose services he might demand and pay for.

But there was a measure of truth in his last accusation. She had not thought of Cassie, and the trust and affection which had begun to grow between them, which she would have shattered abruptly by walking out without a word. In those moments of angry humiliation she had thought only of herself. Was that the best she could do for Joanna's daughter?

I should not be expected to endure that kind of behaviour for anyone's sake, she argued back defensively with herself. *Joanna* would not have expected it of me.

And then, in a quiet corner of her mind, a voice said clearly, Yes, Joanna would. When she wanted something from someone else, she didn't usually stop to wonder if it would be convenient for them!

The thought was so unprecedented, so revolutionary that she could not catch her breath to speak, and she stood there, struggling with an idea that wanted to be born, which she did not wholly understand and found it safer to suppress, watching as Max's expression softened, but not for her.

'She certainly is a beautiful kitten, *piccola*, but I think she would like you to let her run away and play,' he said, rescuing the reluctant animal from his daughter's over-zealous grasp. 'Go along for lunch with Linnet. I am rather scruffy, and must go and clean up.'

Cassie ran a finger along her father's chin, and giggled.

'Ugh, Papà! That's prickly!'

'It is. I'll do something about it,' he promised solemnly. His eyes encountered Linnet's, and in an unwilling flashback of sensation she remembered the hard rasp of his stubbled jaw against the soft skin of her face—remembered, and was hard put not to shiver with pleasure.

'Lunch, Cassie,' she said, with a brisk smile, and as she made her way to the dining-room with the child's hand confidingly clasping hers she could not help but admit that this morning she had fought and lost a battle on several fronts.

She had achieved nothing. Her remonstrations had had no real effect on Max di Angeli, had made him feel no remorse, make no resolutions to change his ways. He, on the other hand, had made a fool of her. Despite her protestations, he was too sexually experienced not to be aware that her reaction to his kisses was not aversion.

Furthermore, he had swiftly and efficiently thwarted her only real means of retaliation, which was to leave at once and without argument. The victory was his. Did it always have to be that way? she wondered bleakly.

Dina looked up from the table as they entered.

'*Ciao*,' she said brightly. 'How very hot it is today! And unfortunately this afternoon I must go to the hair salon and sit under the—how you call it?—drier!' She pulled a face. 'Did you see Max yet?'

'I—er—ran into him briefly,' Linnet said evasively. 'He said he had to shower and then he would be along for lunch.'

Dina nodded sagely. 'There is much work waiting for him in the study. Letters, papers,' she sighed. 'He will not have much time to rest, I think. Did he say anything to you—about what happened at the factory?'

Linnet's face was blank with incomprehension.

'Factory? What factory?' she queried.

Dina gestured vaguely. '*Cara*, I do not—how you say?—meddle in these things. I only know that Max went to Rome suddenly, because there was some trouble at one of the di Angeli factories.'

'I did not even know your family owned factories,' Linnet said, nonplussed.

Dina frowned. 'But of course. We have much business,' she said, staring at Linnet as if she could not believe what she was hearing. 'Companies—all over Europe. And banking...insurance, yes? All kinds of business.' She gave a short laugh, embracing the *palazzo* in a sweeping gesture of her arm. 'All this—how do you think it is kept?'

Linnet's astonishment was far greater, and for a moment the two of them locked gazes across a chasm of misunderstanding.

'I thought...I thought you were just...rich, I suppose,' she mumbled, straining to grasp a concept which was new and quite alien to her, and which, she sensed, threatened to overthrow beliefs and notions deeply entrenched in her mind.

'Rich...*si*.' Dina did not deny it. 'But rich does not mean you sit and do nothing, yes? Business does not look after itself.'

She shrugged. Linnet looked down at the antipasto of mussels and fried breadcrumbs on her plate and knew she could not touch it.

'Then who——' She took a deep breath. 'Who *does* look after it?' But she already knew the answer, and with the knowledge came the stinging realisation of her own naïveté. She had been a prize idiot.

'Why—Max, of course,' Dina Freddi said calmly, as if this truth were self-evident. 'Who else?'

Linnet walked the *fondamente*, the waterside boulevards of Venice, until her feet ached with the heat pulsing upwards from the hot paving-stones. She crossed bridges, cut down small alleys which led to yet smaller ones, traversed dusty squares in forgotten, outlying districts where no tourists penetrated. The relentless sun beat down on her hatless head, her bare arms prickled with incipient sunburn, and she had no idea where she was going.

Her world was in turmoil; she no longer knew what was true or false, black or white, only that she had to adjust to a new and different image of Max di Angeli, quite opposed to the one she had nurtured.

It makes no difference, she told herself stubbornly. He was still the heartless philanderer who had wrecked Joanna's life, even if he did go out and earn his daily *lira*—even if he did run a multi-million-dollar business organisation with ramifications in every part of Europe.

But Joanna—Joanna had implied that he did little but flit from skiing party to beach party, from St Tropez to Gstaad. That was the picture she had been shown, the version she had come here believing.

'No one told me about all these business interests,' she had said lamely to Dina.

'But, my dear—no one knew you did not know!' Dina had laughed incredulously. 'How did you get this crazy idea in your head, I do not understand! I wonder what you think Max is doing all day?'

Linnet dared not enlighten her. She had escaped from the table, pleading a sudden sickness, knowing she must get away before Max turned up. Dina was a dear, but she was not always tactful. Why, Max! Linnet has this so funny idea about you! she could almost hear her crying. She could not face his knowing, mocking glance, his scornful awareness of her stupidity.

She had to go back to the Ca' Favorita eventually, of course, but she had roamed so far, and was still so relatively new to this floating city that it took her a while to find her bearings and retrace her steps. She got back later than she had intended, slipping in the back way, thinking that she had a better chance of getting to her room unobserved. She would have to come down for dinner, but she would be more composed after a shower and a change of clothes.

She was sneaking swiftly across the patio when a tall figure emerged from behind one of the tubbed orange trees.

'I was beginning to think you had got yourself lost again,' said Max di Angeli, a touch of derision in his voice. 'I gather you skipped lunch. Wouldn't it have been more sensible to rest if you felt unwell?'

'I needed some fresh air,' she retorted mutinously. 'Surely I am still allowed out, if only on parole?'

His gaze swept over her, taking in the tired face with its film of hot city dust, the sunburned patches on her shoulders and across her collarbone, the limp fair locks, in need of a reviving wash.

'Oh, very fresh, the streets of Venice on the hottest afternoon of the year so far. And you without even the sense to wear a hat,' he said scathingly. 'I took Cosima to Venice Lido, to the beach. You could have come with us, if we could have found you.'

The sudden coolness of the shady patio with its whispering trees and murmuring fountain, after the blinding sun outside, the stinging sarcasm of his reprimand, and, coming back at her in waves, her own ridiculous misapprehensions, were all at once too much for her. Her knees buckled under her, and she sat down heavily on a stone bench, swaying slightly, the world advancing and retreating alarmingly.

She felt a firm arm around her shoulder, a hand under her chin, steadying her—both his. In no condition to escape him, she was idiotically grateful for the strength which alone prevented her from collapsing.

'Take a deep breath,' Max said calmly, quite gently, still supporting her. 'It is only the heat. It will pass.'

But it didn't—not at once. The patio, the trees, the sky above, all began to whirl and spin frighteningly. Linnet gasped and felt herself falling into an abyss, a bottomless pit without end, down, down... and then, just before the darkness claimed her, she was caught, lifted in a pair of strong arms, and knew, crazily, that she was safe.

She had a vague memory of being in her room, of careful, capable hands—Dina's—undressing her, of being put to bed, of doctors and stethoscopes and whispered conversations. And then she slept.

She awoke later—it had to be much later, because there was a lamp glowing—to find Signora Marchetti sitting beside her bed. Linnet blinked, and was trying to recollect exactly how she had got there when the housekeeper smiled, stood up, rested a hand lightly on her forehead, and went to the door.

'Signor Max,' she called softly.

Linnet groaned, as it all came back to her how she had finally compounded her foolishness by fainting into his arms—it had to have been, there had been no one else there to catch her—and now there he was, standing in the doorway looking quizzically at her.

She struggled up on her pillow, half sitting, hating him seeing her like this, lying there so helpless.

'How do you feel?' he asked, advancing towards the bed. 'The doctor agrees it was mild heatstroke, and advises rest, nothing to eat today, and plenty of fluid.'

He poured a glass of fresh lemon juice from a jug on the bedside table, and actually sat on the edge of her bed to give it to her. Linnet could feel the warmth of his thigh against her own leg, through the thin summer coverlet, and she was uncomfortably aware that her cotton nightdress did not leave much of her shape to the imagination. Not that there was anything sexually arousing about her at this moment, she thought ruefully—she must look about as enticing as a limp lettuce!

'I've never done anything like this before. Fainting, I mean,' she said apologetically.

'There is a first time for everything,' he observed. 'Oddly enough, I was just thinking that it was time we moved to our summer place. The heat has arrived earlier and more fiercely than ever this year.'

Seeing her look of surprised questioning, he said, 'I own a country house in the Veneto, across the lagoon from the city. Venice is just too hot for comfort at the height of summer. There are too many people and not enough green open spaces. There, we have large gardens and our own stretch of beach. You will like it, I think.' He smiled. 'And you need not think you will be deprived of Venice completely. Boat services run regularly across the lagoon.'

His calm solicitude was almost more than she could bear, renewing all her feelings of guilt and stupidity.

'Max—there is something I want to say,' she began hoarsely.

'Tomorrow,' he forestalled her authoritatively. 'For tonight—sleep. *Buona notte*, Linnet.'

With that, he left her, and Linnet, falling back on her pillows, could not suppress a creeping resentment. Tomorrow! She was going to have to tell him that in one respect she had run away with entirely the wrong idea about him. He must be aware of that, if he and Dina communicated at all, but he had not let her say it, and get it over with! Tomorrow would be no easier. For all his apparent surface kindness tonight she had an inescapable suspicion that he was deliberately punishing her by making her wait, keeping her in suspense. In the last moments before exhaustion mercifully claimed her, some old but centuries-wise adage about leopards and spots kept running endlessly through her brain. If it was a warning, it was one she knew she would do well to heed.

Breakfast was brought to her in bed by one of the maids, followed shortly by Dina, smiling but concerned.

'This is very kind, but really there was no need,' Linnet protested. 'I feel fine; in fact I was just about to get up.'

'You may get up when you have eaten, but today you are to rest, and you are not to go out,' Dina said. She laughed. 'Those are not only doctor's orders, but Max's, so you had better not disobey them.'

Linnet groaned. 'Is he very annoyed with me?'

Dina frowned, looking puzzled. 'I think not. Why should he be? But you must take more care in hot sun, Linnet. Your English skin is not used to it.'

'I know. It was very silly of me.' Linnet sighed. Of course, Dina did not know the half. She did not know about the scene in Max's office, Linnet's threatened departure, and Max's ruthless prevention of it. She did not know what an idiot Linnet had made of herself, lecturing him about his playboy lifestyle, unaware that he was running a vast network of international commerce. And Linnet herself was only too conscious that she had yet to face the music about that.

She half hoped he would have made one of his sudden, unexplained disappearances, that some crisis would have arisen that would demand his attention—preferably very far away. But that was cowardly, she knew. Better by far to get it over with, admit she had been, at least in part, mistaken, and hope that he would be magnanimous about it.

Having made this resolution, she showered, washed her hair and slipped on a white dress with short sleeves which covered her sunburned shoulders, a painful reminder of yesterday in more ways than one, and emerged at last from the sanctuary of her room.

'Linnet, Linnet, you are better?' Cassie flung herself into Linnet's arms. 'I drew you a picture—look. It's supposed to be you, but I didn't get the arms and legs right.'

'It's lovely, Cassie,' Linnet said gravely.

'Aunty Dina will take me to dancing class, because Papà says you are not to go out. But can we read some more of *The Wind in the Willows* this afternoon? The bit about Mr Toad and the motor car?'

'We certainly can,' Linnet agreed, wondering ruefully if the whole household were under strict instructions not to let her out. Would she find the great door to the watergate barred if she tried to flout Max's orders? And if she slipped out quietly through the back, in contravention, what punishment would he mete out on her return? Linnet shivered. He was like a prince here, his word absolute, his every wish carried out to the letter.

Part of her itched to disobey, just to make the point that he did not and could not rule her so completely, that his authority did not extend that far. But in a more cautious, reasoning part of her mind she knew it would be foolish to defy him merely for the sake of it. Yesterday, she had inconvenienced the entire household, requiring medical attention and constant care, and it made perfect sense for her to take things easily today. She would probably have done so anyway. She just wished he had not seen fit to make such an issue of it.

She found him alone in the dining-room, Dina having already left with Cassie. He was drinking coffee and reading the financial pages of the newspaper, and he merely glanced up at her briefly and said, '*Buon giorno*,' before going back to his intent study.

Linnet coughed nervously. Still standing, she forced herself to break into his concentration, to draw his attention to herself when really she would much rather it remained where it was.

'May I...may I have a word with you?' she asked hesitantly.

He looked up again, frowning slightly.

'Another one? Your words tend to lead us in strange directions,' he said coolly. 'Well, sit down, Linnet, don't hover. I shall get indigestion from watching you.'

She perched uneasily on the edge of one of the dining-chairs. His manner was not encouraging, and she wished fervently that she could have got this out of the way last night, when he had seemed genuinely concerned and more kindly disposed towards her. This distant, pre-occupied man might almost be someone else entirely.

She gulped and plunged in, there being no escape and no real alternative.

'A lot of what I said to you yesterday in the study was as a result of...of a misunderstanding,' she said. 'I had no idea that you were involved in business. I'm sorry if I got hold of the wrong idea.'

If she had hoped he would graciously accept this apology and be done with it, she was sadly mistaken. His eyes narrowed to azure chips, his mouth tautened to a thin line, as he considered her with what seemed oddly like distaste.

'What puzzles me is how you came by this...misunderstanding,' he said slowly, measuring each word, causing Linnet to quail even more beneath the weight of his displeasure. 'I wonder how you acquired the notion that I spent my life flitting between European capitals for the purpose of...of mere amusement?'

For a horrified moment she had thought that pregnant word 'pleasure' was going to be thrust dangerously between them once again. But the wry emphasis he laid on 'amusement' was scarcely any less embarrassing. And he was pushing dangerously close to the roots of her preconceived idea of him.

'I don't know... I suppose I just assumed... because you're rich...' she lied desperately.

He leaned back slightly in his chair, but his more relaxed stance was not reflected in his eyes, which remained hard and observant.

'Despite what the novelist F. Scott Fitzgerald says, the rich are *not* different,' he said drily. 'At least—not the kind of family I belong to. There *are* those who sit on their country acres, only stirring to swan down to Cannes in summer. But the di Angeli are the descendants of merchant princes. Like the Medici, we built a fortune on finance and shipping and trade in the days when Venice was a republic, some five hundred years ago. It's not in our blood to sit back and contemplate it, rather to make it increase and multiply. Do you understand?'

'I do now,' she said, while at the back of her mind a refrain kept nagging her, But *Joanna* said... A brief rebellion stirring in her, she demanded, 'Are you telling me you don't ski, you don't go to Cap Ferrat, you aren't invited to parties?'

'No,' he said brusquely. 'Indeed I'm not telling you any such thing. I do all of those. And I do other things, too, as you so rightly suspected.' He stared at her hard and directly, giving her no quarter. 'I am a man, after all. I work hard, and I'm entitled to play hard.'

Linnet coloured slightly and looked down, but the level, unemotional voice went on, unsparingly.

'This was going to be the only quiet moment of the morning for me, and instead of reading my paper and drinking my coffee in peace I have to spend it explaining to you things which should have been self-evident, if you had a brain, and used it.'

She gasped, reeling from his words as if he had struck her. 'I don't think——'

'It's obvious you don't.' He turned the newspaper over, showing her, on the front page, an article, complete with a photograph of a damaged building. 'That was our petro-chemical factory, not far from Rome, where an explosion occurred. As you can imagine, there were a number of injuries—not pretty. People in hospital to be visited, compensation to be arranged. Enquiries to be set in motion. Only an hour or two of snatched sleep.' His finger stabbed at the page and then pointed accusingly at her. In the same flat, dispassionate tones, he went on, 'Can you also imagine how pleasant it was to be welcomed home, after all this, with a fatuous and entirely misplaced lecture from some bimbo?'

Linnet had been ready to crumble with shame at the recollection, but this was too much. Her head jerked up, and she glared at him, fury sparking in the wide-spaced grey eyes.

'I am *not* a bimbo!' she protested fiercely.

'No? Then prove it. Think for yourself, Linnet, instead of relying on gossip columns, or whatever source of information you use.'

Standing up, he folded up the newspaper and slapped it down on the table. Then he strode out of the room, but, about to slam the door behind him, he half turned, fixing her with an authoritative stare.

'And don't go out in the sun!' he said sternly.

The reverberations of his cold anger hovered in the room all around her long after he had left. With unsteady hands, Linnet poured herself a cup of coffee and tried to drink it, but it tasted like ashes in her mouth. Nervously, she crumbled a bread roll between her fingers, unable even to contemplate eating it.

It was futile to try and forget his anger. She had to assimilate it, to accept that it had more than a little justification. Her excuse was that she simply had not known any of what she had just learned about his life—and why? Because she had relied solely and trustingly upon what Joanna had told her. And Joanna, her friend, whom she had believed without question, had not been altogether honest in the image she had presented of her husband.

Linnet sighed heavily, struggling to cope with a picture that was not black and white, that contained a myriad complex shades of grey in between. Joanna's nervous collapse had been real—that was beyond doubt. Max must have hurt her. Perhaps it had been an unthinking urge to hit back that had made her describe him as a dissolute libertine? In that state of mind, she would hardly have weighed her words.

The fault was mine for taking it as gospel, Linnet thought soberly. If she had used her eyes and ears, used her brain, as Max had so scathingly suggested she should, she might have learned enough, here in the Ca' Favorita, to avoid making an ass of herself.

Her cheeks flamed as she remembered the tired, unshaven man in his study, fresh from dealing with horror and tragedy, wanting only a bath and some sleep, and instead being confronted by a half-hysterical, self-righteous girl who took him to task for debauchery. No wonder he was angry. No wonder he'd reacted the way he had. Not that that made it right, but she could begin, in part, to understand his behaviour.

She did not see him again until just before dinner, but throughout that long day of enforced idleness she had had plenty of time to think and she had thought of little else. Watching him sip his pre-dinner Campari and soda, she wondered despairingly if there was anything she could safely say, any subject of conversation which would not lead her into a trap of her own making. She was afraid of reawakening his disapproval, which she still felt hovering in the air around her, like a miasma. Walking into the room and finding him alone, without the comforting presence of Dina, had hardly been reassuring, for a start.

'I wonder what's keeping Aunt Dina?' he said, a thread of impatience in his voice hinting that he was not too thrilled with Linnet's sole company either.

'She probably got cajoled into reading a further bedtime chapter of *The Wind in the Willows* to Cassie,' Linnet suggested, forcing a light laugh. 'I've already done my stint, but Cassie is hooked on that book.'

'There are worse obsessions than literature, I suppose,' he said evenly. 'And how about you—do you feel recovered enough to pursue your addiction to tramping around Venice?'

'I'm perfectly well now, thank you, and I will be sure to wear my sunhat if my curfew is lifted,' she said with deliberate primness.

'Don't be ridiculous, Linnet, you are in no sense a prisoner,' he said sharply. 'Furthermore, I appreciate your love of the city. It's for people like you, as much as for the inhabitants, that I spent all morning in a stuffy room arguing about rising water levels and restoring fourteenth-century brickwork.'

She raised her eyebrows curiously, but said nothing, fearful of once again jumping to a wrong conclusion, and he permitted himself the faintest of smiles, as if well aware of the reasons for her caution.

'The Venice in Peril Committee,' he informed her. 'We find ways to protect and restore this marvellous living heritage of ours, and of raising funds for the purpose.

I expect you heard about the American journalist who, on arrival here, cabled his editor saying, ''Streets full of water. Please advise''? Well, it's no longer a joke. Increasingly often, the lagoon floods, and we get water where we don't want it, damaging the fabric and interior of ancient buildings. Venice is sinking—albeit very slowly.'

Linnet's eyes widened.

'But that can't be allowed to happen—it must be saved for the future!' she cried.

The gaze resting on her had softened slightly.

'It isn't only the water. It's toxic waste, air pollution—and the more subtle destruction caused simply by too many people coming here all at once,' he said. 'There are immense problems. But I haven't given up hope, and there are many others who are equally concerned, and have the will and the means to act.'

Over the rim of his glass he watched her, relaxed but unmoving. Linnet swallowed hard as yet another piece of the complicated puzzle that was Max di Angeli fell into place. But, far from making it easier for her understanding, she found herself wading into ever deeper and more difficult waters.

Max di Angeli, the demon playboy, the destroyer of women, him she could understand and hate with a vengeance, whole-heartedly and straightforwardly. But Max the concerned and workaholic tycoon, Max the dedicated patron of the arts and protector of his city's future—could she hate him with quite such honest fervour? And if hatred was denied her, how was she supposed to feel about him?

Either her dilemma was written on her face, or he was, as she had so often feared, something of a mind-reader.

Reaching out and tipping back her chin with the long, flexible fingers of one hand, he chuckled softly.

'Don't get too carried away with remorse, little songbird,' he chuckled wryly. 'I shouldn't like you to start thinking of me as a plaster saint instead of a devil. I've been playing polo all afternoon, and tonight I have another... engagement.'

His fingers traced just the lightest path along her throat—she couldn't have called it a caress—and then left her. To her astonished mortification, she realised that she had been holding her breath, waiting for it to develop into exactly that, willing his touch to become deeper, harder, wanting to feel the deliberate, sensual pressure of his hands on her. How could she? How *could* she?

But he merely refilled his glass and said casually, 'I hope you have brought a swimsuit or two along. If not, you had better go out and buy yourself some. We're leaving for the country at the weekend.'

Linnet couldn't answer, couldn't speak. She could only nod mutely. What was happening to her? What was this strange, incredible sensation that inflamed her at his slightest, most casual touch, making her aware of herself, her body, her womanhood, in a way she had never known before? Months in this household stretched ahead of her, long months in which she must endure and suppress and conceal these feelings—in which they could surely only grow stronger, until her feeble defences were no longer a match for them.

And then?

CHAPTER FIVE

THE country mansion of the di Angeli family lay among the lush, flat green countryside of the long arm that curved around the lagoon, opposite the island on which Venice itself was situated.

Linnet observed that not only water separated them from the Ca' Favorita, but that architecturally they had moved forwards several centuries from the Middle Ages to the Classical period. The house was pure Palladian, elegant and symmetrical, with a portico at the front entrance supported by graceful white columns, and all the elevations planned on clean, spare lines. At the front there were formal gardens with carefully tended flower-beds, fountains, statuary and ornamental ponds. At the back was a more casual grassed area, with trees and a tennis court. There was no swimming-pool—it wasn't necessary, since the whole backed on to a private beach, shelving gently into the glassy, shimmering blue waters of the Adriatic.

Gianni had taken their luggage round the long way by road, via Jessolo. Linnet, Cassie and Dina had caught the boat from the frantically busy quay at Riva degli Schiavoni, where traders set up stalls selling handbags and jewellery, and tourists jostled with the passengers disgorging from the many boats that plied the lagoon. Gianni met them with the car at Punta Sabbioni, where the service terminated, and drove them the short way to the house.

As with the Ca' Favorita, no expense had been spared here, Linnet could see instantly, with eyes that were now used to assessing and appreciating quality. But it was lighter, airier, with the ambience of a summer retreat, more windows admitting more daylight, paler colours, more modern furnishings, less mystery. Her room here was enormous, more like a suite, and only the fact that she had become accustomed to living in palatial splendour prevented her from gasping at the spaciousness of her quarters.

There was, of course, a formal dining-room, but they lunched out on a sunny terrace protected from the heat by a vine-covered pergola, where refreshing breezes drifted in from the sea.

'Can we go to the beach now? Please, please!' Cassie was beside herself with excitement. Linnet glanced at Dina, who nodded.

'You go. I am going to put up my feet and read a novel,' she declared.

Linnet rose with a smile. 'All right—come along. But no swimming until our lunch has settled. OK?'

It was strange to lie on a beach and know that you had it all to yourself, so no one could run past and kick sand in your face, or turn up their ghetto-blaster just as you were dropping off to sleep. But Linnet was not used to this sequestered privacy. She could hear the distant shouts and laughter of holiday-makers on the public beach, and could not make up her mind if she liked her privileged status or would rather be with the crowd.

'Has lunch settled now? Can we go in?' Cassie was impatient to be in the sea. Linnet, in a turquoise one-piece swimsuit she had bought the previous summer, waded into the water, carefully watching the little girl to see how good a swimmer she was, and how much actual supervision was required. She need not have worried. Cassie swam like a fish, and the sea was warm and calm with scarcely a ripple. After a while, she got out, dried herself off, put on more sun-oil and contented herself with watching from the beach as Cassie splashed and ducked happily.

'Basting yourself thoroughly, I see.'

She had not heard his soft footfall on the sand, and the first she saw of Max was when he flopped down easily beside her. The sight of his long, firm body in swimming-shorts threw her into pink-faced confusion as she tried not to be aware of the tanned, muscular legs and chest, the flat, athletic stomach, the line of dark hair across the pectorals. He was one of those fortunate men who looked as good undressed as in an expensive suit, a living declaration that clothes did *not* make the man.

'You've missed a bit,' he said, taking the bottle of oil out of her limply unresisting hand. And then his hand was smoothing oil over her neck and shoulders, and down as far as the low-cut back of her swimsuit. The light but firm pressure made her spine tingle deliciously, the sensitive nerves radiating out from it springing to life and sending messages of incredible delight all over her body—down her arms and legs, spreading round to her stomach and shooting up into her breasts, an intense, concentrated excitement she had never felt before.

She wanted it to continue, to go on and on, wanted the experienced, knowledgeable hands to explore and excite her even more. For she knew instinctively there was much more than this; pleasurable as it was, it was only a beginning.

Was this the way he had made Joanna feel? And look how it had ended for her!

The sudden stiffening of her body must have communicated itself to him. His hands rested, all at once still, on her shoulders, and then he removed them completely.

'You should get a bikini, Linnet,' he remarked lazily. 'You could tan more that way. Especially with the top off.'

The waves of heat rippling through her body had nothing to do with the sun's warmth.

'I don't sunbathe topless,' she said, knowing her voice sounded unbearably priggish.

'No?' She only heard the shrug in his voice, since she was carefully avoiding his eyes. 'A lot of girls do these days, although in my opinion it becomes rather boring on the beach, when there's so much on display. But we are private here. You could strip off with impunity.'

Not with you around, I couldn't, she thought fervently, not daring to think what it would be like to expose even more of herself to his coolly appreciative gaze. Feeling deeply hypocritical, in view of her body's unthinking and primitive response, she said, 'I'd rather not, thank you.'

'*Va bene*' he said, with casual indifference. 'I'm going for a swim. This is my only afternoon of self-indulgence for some days to come.'

She watched as he swam and played in the water with Cassie for a while, but somehow felt shy of joining them. She was not part of the family, not really. She felt that Cassie, while she had her father, did not need her, and Max did not issue any invitation. When they came out, Cassie dozed off, curled up under the sun umbrella, and Max sat letting the sun's rays, now past their fiercest heat, dry his already magnificently tanned body.

'Cassie is a superb little swimmer,' Linnet remarked, 'but what she really needs is some other children to play with. She won't meet them on a private beach.'

He shot her a warning look.

'I'm particular whom my daughter makes friends with,' he said. 'When she starts school she will have plenty of suitable companions.'

'And until then? Didn't your wife's friends ever bring their families for an afternoon on the beach?'

He laughed shortly. 'Joanna's friends, if they had the inconvenience of children, usually made sure they had nannies to leave them with,' he said drily. 'Cosima is singularly lucky in that she has always had Dina on hand.'

Linnet did not miss the sharp note in his voice, which might have warned her to tread no further along this particular path, but she could not prevent herself.

'I thought all Italians were crazy about children,' she said, as casually as possible, as if it were mere polite conversation, and she had no deeper interest in Joanna's life here.

'For the most part,' he agreed. 'But my wife's circle were mostly expatriate English or Americans. She never became fluent enough in Italian to have a really close Italian friend.'

'In seven years?' Linnet said, so shocked that she spoke without thinking.

The blue eyes were veiled and narrowed as he stared hard at her.

'Who told you how long I had been married?' he demanded.

'Why. . . I suppose Dina must have done,' Linnet said quickly. She was cold now—unreasonably, for the sun was still pleasantly warm—cold and afraid. She had touched the outer edges of the dark mystery that was Max and Joanna's marriage, and its dead, icy fingers had brushed her own sensitive spirit. 'Surely it's not a secret?'

'No, it isn't,' he conceded. 'But I'd rather not discuss my marriage, and I would be grateful if you didn't talk about it with my aunt. She and Joanna did not get on too well, anyhow.'

Linnet found this hard to believe. Dina was so friendly and open, so helpful, that it was difficult to imagine anyone not finding her congenial. And Joanna...Joanna could charm anyone, convulse a room with her wit, brighten any gathering with her smile...

Just as long as she was getting her own way, said that quiet, unknown voice again, and Linnet started, as if it were sitting on her shoulder, whispering unpleasant truths in her unwilling ear. No—go away, she exhorted it. Joanna is dead; it's not fair... And the voice said, Come on, now, she could be moody and bitchy and plain bloody-minded if something didn't suit her...

Linnet could not bear to ask herself where it came from, this voice, and why she was hearing it only now, since she had been here in Italy. Instead, shaking her head vigorously, she said, 'I assure you, I would not dream of discussing your marriage. It's no business of mine, and really only concerns me where it touches on Cassie.'

His reply was hard, cynical, a flat denial that forbade her to probe further.

'It touches on her scarcely at all,' he said. 'That much I can promise you.'

* * *

It seemed to Linnet that she was living two different lives. One was calm and peaceful and almost routine, the pleasant, unexceptional existence which was the pattern of her days when Max was away. At such times, she nearly persuaded herself that she was content, that all was well and that she was quite at home in the di Angeli ménage. Except for the fact that she was living in such a luxurious and beautiful environment, and that Cassie was a wealthy and slightly over-protected child, it was not essentially different from family life anywhere.

Days could pass like this, when she was all but convinced, lulled by sea, sun and habit, pleased by the rapid improvement in her use of the Italian language, growing increasingly fond of Cassie. And then, suddenly, Max would return from wherever business had taken him, and at once everything was different.

Not that the pattern changed. The tenor of the household was brisker for the presence of its head, but she knew that the difference was chiefly in herself. She was unable to relax, found it hard to behave normally, knowing that he was around. Simply the knowledge that he might be in for dinner, that he might suddenly appear on the beach or in the gardens cast her into a frenzy of anticipation.

She had to admit that it was no longer merely apprehension in case she had unwittingly transgressed in some way, or fear that a slip of the tongue might betray some fact that she should really have no means of knowing. She had to admit to herself honestly, since she could no longer seriously deny it, that he attracted her.

He had married her friend, made her desperately unhappy, and finally driven her to a breakdown. This Linnet knew. She could not pretend it had not happened. And still she was attracted to him. She could offer no excuses. This was a man with a powerful physical charm, and she was no more immune to it than Joanna had been. Her best, her only hope was to work out these next months without giving him the amusement of realising it.

One evening he went into Venice for a dinner engagement and was not at the table for breakfast. Dina, quite unperturbed, sitting there with her coffee and rolls and fruit juice, smiled thoughtfully at Linnet.

'He is a grown man, you know, and does not have to tell everyone of his comings and goings.'

'I didn't say anything,' Linnet replied quickly.

'You did not have to, *cara*. It is on your face that you do not approve,' Dina said gently.

'It's not my business,' Linnet insisted stubbornly. 'Only... his wife has not been dead very long, has she? Isn't it a little soon to be seeking... consolation?'

'Ah.' Dina paused, then shook her head expressively. 'We do not know this is what he is doing. You are jumping to...'

'Conclusions,' Linnet supplied.

'*Si*. Conclusions. But, even if what you are thinking is true, men have needs, do they not?'

'Women have them too,' Linnet said unthinkingly, and Dina nodded in complete agreement.

'This is true. I was married for many years. Now I am alone, I miss... the closeness,' she admitted wistfully. 'But for women the feelings are more for one man, a special man, one who is loved. Do you have someone like that?'

It was Linnet's turn to shake her head.

'Not one particular one, no,' she said. 'I was always too busy studying, too wrapped up in music. There was never time to think of it. But I don't believe a man can easily forget or replace a special woman either. If Max cared about his wife——'

She stopped herself abruptly, realising that she was doing exactly what he had forbidden her to do—discussing his marriage. It was not only her own uneasy conscience, but the sudden closed, guarded look on Dina's usually open face that pulled her up.

'I'm sorry,' she apologised quickly. 'As I said, it's none of my business.'

Dina put a sympathetic hand briefly on Linnet's arm. 'You live here, as part of our family. It is natural you want to know things,' she said. 'If I tell you . . . between us, as friends . . . that this marriage was never ideal, and by the end was not really a marriage at all . . . can we then say no more? Max is not an easy man, I know; he is demanding, too handsome for his own good, and always on the move. But Joanna——' She hesitated a long moment, and Linnet was almost afraid to exhale for fear of distracting her.

Finally, she said unwillingly, as if it was being drawn from her, 'Joanna was difficult. From the start, I don't think she liked Italy. Always she was going away, and coming back, and going away again. Buying clothes in Paris, visiting friends in Cannes.'

Joanna going away? *Joanna* absenting herself from the household? For so long Linnet had carried around this sad picture of Joanna as a virtual prisoner in the Ca' Favorita, at the mercy of her husband's caprice, that she could scarcely believe what Dina was telling her.

She's Max's aunt, naturally she's biased in his favour, she thought, but she could not in all good faith deny that Dina was an honest, straightforward individual. And she readily admitted Max's faults.

'But surely all that changed when Cassie was born?' she said.

'I hoped—I crossed my fingers,' Dina said. 'A child can sometimes hold a man and a woman together. But——' She shook her head again. 'I am already saying too much. Is enough,' she said with finality.

Joanna must have been so unhappy, Linnet told herself forcefully, that not even her child could make life good for her. She had to keep running away. It had to have been Max who had done this to her...

But her once unswerving conviction was beginning to shake a little. The picture was no longer the pure, untarnished, one-dimensional image she'd held firmly in her mind when she'd come to Venice. Fresh perspectives were appearing, new angles she had not suspected. And however strongly she kept insisting to herself that this must be nonsense—after all, she had *known* Joanna—even there, an element of doubt had begun to creep in. How well could a naïve, adolescent girl really know a young woman several years her senior, a woman already in full possession of her sexual identity?

Linnet felt herself crowded and unsettled by all these doubts and questions, and since Dina had gone visiting, taking Cassie with her, there was no one to distract her from them. The day was as unfailingly hot and sunny as ever, but she could raise no enthusiasm for the prospect of lying on the beach alone.

I'll go out, she decided briskly. She had long been promising herself a trip to the islands in the Venetian lagoon—here was her chance.

Changing into black Bermuda shorts, a white sun-top and sandals—not forgetting her floppy sunhat—she caught the bus which passed along the main road to

Treporti, from where the boats to the islands left at regular intervals.

It was pleasant to sit on the little steamer's open upper deck, letting the breeze stream through her long hair, watching interestedly as Burano hove gradually closer, picking out the tall campanile of its church, then a jumble of houses, and last the quay, where she jumped eagerly ashore.

It was incredibly, unbelievably picturesque, almost a parody of itself, and gave Linnet the feeling she had often experienced in Venice—that some crazily inspired film director had deliberately gone over the top in flinging together all these elements to create a set. As in Venice, Burano was intersected by canals, but in spite of a number of people wandering the narrow alleys, bridges and waterside pathways a dreamily peaceful air pervaded it. The narrow houses were all painted, not in pastels but in deep, vibrant colours—teal-blue, vermilion, dark olive-green—and outside each one was moored a small boat, the only means of transport on this watery island.

Entranced, Linnet strolled along, pausing to gaze in at shop windows where women were painstakingly making the lace for which Burano was famed. Turning down a canalside street bordered by restaurants, she found herself facing the church, and a large square with a market in full swing.

Black-shawled old women were buying their vegetables amid the tourists haggling over glass animals and lace mats, and there, as unexpected and unbelievable as a mirage, was Max di Angeli, tall and instantly noticeable, with one arm around the bowed shoulders of one such woman, actually carrying her wicker shopping basket.

Linnet came to a dead halt in the middle of the street, aware that she was staring openly, and unable to do anything about it. He hadn't seen her, anyhow. He was laughing, and so was the old lady—in fact, she was cackling heartily, and Linnet saw her affectionately slap him on the thigh, as if they had just shared a rather racy joke.

She watched this little scene with growing disbelief, but it *really* was Max, although what he was doing here, and in such company, she could not imagine. Whatever it was, she thought she should not be caught observing him, and was about to scuttle back down the street and into one of the shops when, still laughing, he turned and looked straight at her.

Linnet froze. There was no way she could now disappear, or pretend she had not seen him. Besides, she told herself, straightening up, she had done nothing wrong. It was not as if she had followed him, or even known he would be here, so why was she once again feeling guilty?

'Linnet.' He called to her, and although his tone was casual it was a summons, and she answered it, going slowly towards where he stood.

'*Buon giorno*.' She nodded politely to the old lady, who was looking up at her with alert, interested eyes. Linnet listened carefully as Max explained who she was, picking up, in spite of the fluid swiftness of his speech, that she was English and helping to look after Cosima. But she caught very little of the reply, except a phrase suggesting that Max was always a naughty little boy, and thank God he was a bit better now!

'Alba was my nanny, more years ago than I care to remember,' Max said with a smile. 'She came originally from Burano, and finally retired to live here again.'

Linnet smiled acknowledgement as Alba retrieved her shopping basket, wished them *arrivederci* and scurried off to join a group of her cronies at one of the stalls.

Alone with Max again—even though there were plenty of people around his presence was such that she always felt alone with him, even in a crowd—Linnet said, 'Dina has taken Cassie to visit someone, so I took the opportunity to do some sightseeing.'

'You don't have to answer to me for what you do in your free time,' he said. He still wore the trousers of the casual suit in which he had gone out last night, although he had discarded the tie, rolled up the shirt sleeves, and carried the jacket over his arm.

'I thought you were in Venice,' she said.

'I don't have to answer to you for what I do in my free time,' he replied, and she flushed. 'Joke, Linnet,' he said, and, looking up, she saw that he was grinning. Then he said, 'Well, I'll tell you. Last night's dinner party was so boring that I made an excuse, left early, hopped on a boat and came to see Alba. By the time we had finished a bottle of wine and talked a lot, I'd missed the last boat, so she put me up—telling me off for being a naughty boy all the while!'

'She was obviously only too delighted to see you,' Linnet remarked carefully, absorbing all this. Max di Angeli, going out to a sophisticated dinner party and ending up visiting his old nanny—and evidently with great mutual affection and enjoyment.

'I should hope so. Alba was like a mother to me,' he said with deep and unexpected fervour. 'My real mother died when I was small, and I saw far less of my father than Cosima sees of me. In fact, he was no more than a remote figure. It was Alba who listened to my troubles and bathed my grazed knees, and got me out of fights when she could. She was my anchor.'

His voice was very quiet and sober, and Linnet did not doubt that he was telling her the truth, not only about his rather sad childhood, but about what he had done last night. If only it were always this simple, if she could always trust him to be straightforward and unequivocal, without the lurking depths which lay in wait to disconcert her.

'Why so serious? If you're pitying me for being a deprived child, save your sympathy,' he said, half facetiously. 'I had the best of everything, practically and educationally, and I was my father's sole heir.'

'There are other ways of being deprived,' she observed, but he merely smiled, and suddenly and surprisingly took her hand.

'Hunger is the only one I'm conscious of right now,' he said firmly. Glancing at the line of restaurants with adjacent terraces full of diners dedicatedly watching each other, he said, 'This would be too much like being in a zoo. I know somewhere quieter, where the food is excellent.'

Linnet was so bemused by his cheerful, and for once unsarcastic manner that she did not protest as he led her across a bridge and down a quiet alley. It seemed deserted, with no possibility of there being a restaurant anywhere near, but he turned under an archway and shepherded her along a dim passage which opened into a tiny courtyard.

There were no more than half a dozen tables, two of which were occupied, covered by pink and white checked cloths. Thick vines smothered the walls, bees droned lazily round tubs of brilliant flowers, and the whole was open to the cloudless blue sky above.

'There's no menu,' Max told Linnet as a smiling girl led them to a table. 'You just take what there is. It's always good.'

He was right. First they were served rissoles of spinach and ricotta cheese, followed by something Linnet did not recognise.

'*Fiori di zucchini*,' Max laughed at her puzzlement. 'Deep-fried courgette flowers. Go ahead—they're perfectly edible. Look.' He popped one into his mouth, ate it, and watched as she did the same, finding them delicate and delightfully tasty.

The main course was a splendid *brodetti* or fish stew, brimming with squid, clams, as well as all kinds of fish, and flavoured with saffron and tomatoes. White wine came with it, in a plain earthenware jug, and a small basket of bread rolls completed the meal.

'That was wonderful!' Linnet exclaimed, almost too replete for comfort. 'But imagine—if someone didn't happen to like fish!'

'Ah—you have to be adventurous and fairly eclectic in your eating habits,' Max said. 'Places like this are not for the faint-hearted and fussy.'

'Did you come here with your wife?' she heard herself asking, astonishing herself that she should even dare to introduce the subject when he was in such a sunny mood. But for once his brow did not darken at the mention of her.

'Joanna? Lord, no—far too down-market for her,' he said unworriedly. 'With Joanna it had to be the Gritti Palace or nothing. Now—what's next? Yes, Linnet, you certainly can manage to dispose of a simple *granita all' arancia*.'

She did, since it was only water-ice, but tasting superbly of freshly squeezed oranges. You pushed your

luck there, she told herself, bringing Joanna into it, and somehow you got away with it.

Meeting her eyes across their second cup of excellent coffee, he said, 'Life is strange, isn't it?'

'How do you mean?' She hoped the tremor in her voice was well disguised.

'For instance.' He toyed idly with the sugar spoon. 'Here you are, sitting in a restaurant on Burano, instead of studying with Maestro Donetti. Looking after my daughter instead of singing Verdi or Mozart. A year ago, could either of us ever have imagined it?'

'No,' she said quietly. A year ago, she was still singing. The tragedy that had imperilled her voice had not yet struck. A year ago, Joanna was still alive. He had not known he would soon be a widower. But here they were, as he had said. Linnet felt suddenly and pulsingly full of life, spilling over with it, half guilty for nurturing such vibrant feelings, and ridiculously thankful at the same time.

So she still could not sing, and who knew if she ever would? But she was alive, and here with this man, eating good, simple food under a blue sky, the sun warm on her back.

'It must have been an awful blow to you, putting the brakes on your career like that,' he said. 'Obviously you were good, for Donetti to have accepted you as a pupil.'

She gave a shrug.

'At the time, I was devastated. I can only wait and hope, and meanwhile try not to dwell on it,' she said. 'There are worse tragedies that can befall people.'

She did not enlarge on this, but he must have guessed what she was referring to.

'I'll tell you something for free, Linnet,' he said in a strange voice, quiet, yet charged with controlled emotion.

'We can most of us cope with the major catastrophes of life when they are thrown at us. The harder test is accepting the missed opportunities, the things that don't work out as we dreamed or expected. The miscalculations. Being wrong. That's what hurts the most.'

He signalled to the waitress, and piled notes and coins on to the plate she carried. '*Molto grazie*.'

Linnet watched this transaction without a word. She was still digesting his, and there was nothing she would have dared to add, certainly nothing she would have dared to ask. The day had already been full of surprises, from Dina's revelations that morning to a delightful lunch with this unexpectedly pleasant and charming companion. And now it was a tricky enough task working out what he meant, let alone risking commenting on it.

His deep, alluring smile illuminated his face as he turned back to her.

'End of today's lecture,' he said, deliberately self-mocking. 'A short walk is a good way to work off excessive indulgence and a tendency to over-seriousness.'

They strolled back along the canalside walks to the quay, but the boat was not due in yet, so they walked on, past a grassy area with trees and iron benches, to a part of the island that was like a little piece of wild countryside, with tall grass and birdsong and solitude.

Max sat down, gazing out over the wide blue expanse of the lagoon, and after a brief hesitation Linnet sat beside him. Everything was quiet, and they might have been the only two people on the island...or in the world. And perhaps for the first time Linnet felt at ease with him, as if a barrier had been reached and crossed.

'Peaceful moments like this are pretty rare,' he said, uncannily reading her thoughts. 'Especially for you and me, Linnet, huh?'

He half turned towards her and reached out a hand, brushing her cheek as he lifted a long tress of her hair. Then he let it go, and his hand rested on her shoulder where the sunburned skin of that traumatic day had healed and begun to peel slightly.

'Little songbird who flew too near the sun, like Icarus,' he said softly, his fingers slipping down towards her breast.

Linnet watched the progress of his hand, transfixed, almost unable to breathe. She was full of an aching sensation, waiting for his hand to close over the rounded softness, desiring it with all her being. Her eyes closed, and the summer air hummed expectantly all around her.

The blast of a ship's horn split the air.

'I forgot,' he said lightly. 'You don't like being touched, do you? Or so you would have me believe. Come along. The boat's in. Let's go home.'

CHAPTER SIX

THEIR arrival back together caused no comment, only a brief lifting of Dina's eyebrows.

'Look who I ran into on Burano,' Max said casually.

Dina smiled. 'You went to see Alba, I expect? How did you find her?'

'Well. Getting older, naturally, but otherwise unchanged. She gave me a good telling-off for nothing in particular, but I suppose I must have deserved it somewhere down the line.'

His voice was wry, but Dina said laughingly, 'You know she worships the ground you walk on. You have too much appeal for women of all ages, Max. I only wish you would use it more sparingly.'

'Oh, I don't think Alba is over-impressed by my charms. To her, I'm still the little boy she used to spank,' he replied airily.

But Linnet had caught the warning note in his aunt's voice, and also the quick glance she had cast in her direction. What was she saying? Don't allow this little English girl to become infatuated with you—it would be unfair to her?

Looking in her dressing-table mirror a little later, Linnet saw that her cheeks were pink, her eyes were shining. It could have been the effect of the sun and the breeze as she'd stood on the steamer's deck with Max by her side. But it could also have been a result of the lingering sensations caused by the leisurely lunch and the wine, the unexpected closeness, and the brief but deeply affecting touch of his hand. She looked dreamy and sensual—like a woman who had just made love. Or wanted to.

Linnet jumped up, shocked by the explicit eroticism of her own thoughts. Even thinking about Max making love to her was dangerous, never mind actively desiring it, fantasising about it, wondering how it would feel. She had to stop this!

She had been a quiet child and a shy adolescent, and all her life had taken it for granted that she was rather a cerebral person. Only music had released her capacity for passion; only when she'd sung had she felt gloriously alive and fulfilled. So why, now, was she becoming more aware, day by day, of her physical self, her body's needs and responses? Was it because she couldn't sing? Was that the trigger that had catapulted this other, unsuspected side of her nature to the forefront?

Perhaps it would have happened anyhow, if her path had crossed that of Max di Angeli. If she had met him somehow while she was a pupil of Maestro Donetti, maybe she would still have been unable to resist becoming addicted to his frighteningly seductive charm.

I must not let this happen to me, she told herself firmly; I must resist it, with all my strength, with all my power. Finding him attractive was bad enough, but today, listening to him talk about his childhood, she had been aware of the dawnings of sympathy. From there, it was one short step to starting to care about him . . . to falling in love.

No, no, and no again! She had her whole life ahead of her; one day soon she would sing again—she *had* to. She would not allow herself to be bruised and possibly destroyed by a foolish romantic attachment to an amoral man who at best might make casual love to her, out of a moment's curiosity, and then go his way.

In spite of all these stern instructions to herself she could not help taking great care dressing for dinner, choosing a dress she knew looked good, brushing her long hair until it shone, and she could hardly wait for the moment to arrive when she could go downstairs.

He was standing on the terrace, glass in hand, gazing out at the sun setting over the lush, serene countryside, and he turned towards her as she came out.

'Ah, Linnet,' he said, and his tone was so brisk and businesslike that it made her start. 'I'm glad you have come down a little early. It gives me a chance to speak to you in private.'

Something about his voice, his entire manner chilled her. In private? They had spent most of the afternoon together, to all intents and purposes. What did he have to say now that he could not have said then? Had Dina's warning got through to him, and was he about to caution her not to read too much into what was only a lunch...? Linnet went cold with shame. No, she cried inwardly, don't tarnish the memory of that lovely afternoon. I *know* that's all it was!

'I shall be giving a dinner party next week—on the Friday evening,' he said. 'There will be people coming who are important to me, for one reason or another, so I expect it to be a success—you understand?'

'Yes——' Linnet said slowly. Was this the same man who had smiled at her across the pink-checked table a few hours earlier? Who was now addressing her in this flat, employer-like monotone? 'Yes, I understand, but where do I come into it?'

'Sit down, have a drink, and I'll explain it to you.' He gestured her swiftly to a chair, but she did not feel any more at ease, seated and with a glass in her hand, nor did his demeanour become noticeably warmer.

'I want you to help Dina with the arrangements. This has been a hard year for her, and although she doesn't show it I know she is tired. But please be unobtrusive about it. I don't want her to get the mistaken idea that I don't believe her perfectly capable. Do you think you can do that, in addition to looking after Cosima?'

'Of course I can,' she said promptly, almost relieved that this was all he had to say, even though she was hurt by the coolness of his tone. 'Haven't I already told you that in my opinion I am under-employed? I'll be glad to help. Your staff are marvellous, anyhow, and I do know about these things—I was brought up in a hotel!'

'That's what I reckoned on,' he said levelly. 'You will have my gratitude.'

'I don't need your gratitude, Max,' she said quietly, stung that he should even offer it. 'I only wish I had known sooner. There must be lots of ways in which I could lighten Dina's load, and I prefer to be useful.'

Her voice matched his for cool impersonality, but inwardly she was crying. Why? This afternoon, they had been almost friends. Why couldn't he have approached her on that basis? Why this reversion to the cautious, guarded atmosphere of her early days at the Ca' Favorita?

'Good,' he said briskly. 'That's settled.' He looked her over, a formal appraisal such as he might have given goods in a shop window. 'I shall expect you to be present at dinner as well, naturally.'

'Is that...will that be necessary?' she demurred. 'I mean, I'm only an employee——'

'Linnet.' He stopped her with a frown and an upturned hand. 'Enough. You should know that half the hard work of these occasions is on the actual night. So be there, prepared to be charming. And buy yourself a new dress. You can send me the bill.'

'There's no need. You pay me more than adequately, and I've hardly spent any of it,' she retorted proudly.

'Let's not have this silly argument all over again,' he said, a bored expression on his face. 'The plain fact is that the women will all be wearing designer clothes. You know what I mean? I don't want you to look or feel out of place.'

All the care she had taken with her appearance that evening, the dress she had so painstakingly chosen, and felt so good in, it was all reduced to nothing. She might as well have been sitting there dressed in a dustbin liner! How could he have admired how she looked, when he was used to expensively dressed women who bought their clothes from top couture establishments? She remembered Joanna's copper-coloured leggings and tunic, the day she had driven over to see her for the last time. The outfit had looked so simple and elegant, she had not given a thought to what it must have cost. She knew now that that kind of understated chic cost a good deal of money. She knew now that to the women of Max's acquaintance her own wardrobe was no more than cheap tat!

But he didn't have to point this out to her quite so mercilessly. He didn't have to make her feel quite so small! And to think this afternoon she had almost liked him! That should teach me a lesson, she thought grimly, sipping mechanically at her Campari without tasting it, watching the red sun dissolve splendidly into a lilac dusk, and seeing nothing of its beauty.

'I'm supposed to be at this dinner party Max is having next Friday,' Linnet said casually to Dina later. 'I really can't see why.'

'But of course you will be there,' Dina said at once, ruling out any hope of help from that quarter. 'You live here! What do you think—you should stay in your room like the governess in that Victorian novel... *Jane Eyre*, or something?'

Linnet laughed uneasily. The analogy was uncomfortable, since the eponymous Jane had fallen heavily for her employer, with disastrous consequences!

'Perhaps not. But if I'm going to be there maybe I could help with the preparations? It would be interesting for me,' she suggested. 'Honestly, Dina, I don't have nearly enough to do around here.'

'*Va bene*.' Dina shrugged. 'If you like. We make lists, plan table, plan menus, *si*? You like arranging flowers?'

'Very much. I used to do the dining-room arrangements quite often in my parents' hotel. I'd jump at the chance to do the same thing here.'

'I put you in charge of that, then. Use whatever you want from the gardens and greenhouses, and buy what else you need. It must be good.'

'It will be,' Linnet promised a little shakily, praying that this long-unused skill had not deserted her. 'The guests... are they business associates of Max's?'

'Some, yes, and also some members of the family from far away. There will be an... *amica*... friend of Max, also, I think.'

Something meaningful in her tone, and the fact that Dina had used the word '*amica*', Italian being quite explicit about the gender of the friend, alerted Linnet's attention.

'A woman friend? Someone special? It's a...a bit soon for that, isn't it?'

'Oh, come.' Dina shrugged tolerantly. 'Max is attractive man in the fullness of life. He should not live alone, like a bachelor. In Italy, that is not considered to be good. A man should have a wife...a family.'

'And there are already candidates?' Linnet tried to keep her voice light.

'Many *mammas* with unmarried daughters are very—interested to see him free again,' Dina said shrewdly. 'He maybe should, how do you say, consider what they have to offer. If he had been guided by his father the first time, instead of marrying this girl from England—admittedly from good family, but so different in outlook—well, maybe it is better my brother not live to see how it ended.'

'Perhaps he fell in love,' Linnet suggested, but Dina merely sniffed.

'It is not for me to say, but I suspect the main reason was to rebel against his father,' she remarked. 'This time, now he is older and wiser, perhaps he will be guided by sense.'

Linnet judiciously decided not to comment any further, but the knowledge that a woman who might be important to Max would be one of the guests radically altered her own attitude, and all at once she did not want to look the part of the poor but respectable governess!

Not without trepidation she caught the boat to Venice and braved the fashionable boutiques to the north of the Piazza San Marco, shops inside whose dim, hallowed interiors she had never ventured before. The prices made her catch her breath. It felt positively wicked spending so much on one outfit, but she forced herself to take the plunge, and came back the owner of a simple but stunning lace suit in the mingled colours of autumn leaves—bronze and gold and subtle browns, together with a pair of gold leather pumps and some Byzantium-inspired gold earrings.

There would be twelve around the table, and the guest-list ran like a cosmopolitan *Who's Who*.

'Graf *und* Gräfin Helmut von Rudesdorf,' Linnet read faintly.

'Oh—Rudi? He's a very influential German industrialist,' Dina told her matter-of-factly. 'His wife, the countess, is immensely wealthy in her own right. Now then—who else? Oh, yes—Arturo de Reyes. Cousin Arturo, he's related to us through the Spanish branch of the family. Werner Passewald, he's a Swiss banker.'

'Gracious,' Linnet said, half fearfully, wondering what on earth she would find to say to all these powerful and no doubt highly educated people. And in what language? 'I'm going to be a bit lost. Aside from English, the bit of Italian I've learned here, and my rusty school French, I can't speak anything else——' she began.

'Please don't worry. With so many different nationalities, we shall probably all be speaking English, which everyone knows, more or less,' Dina assured her. 'And you are a very lovely and interesting person, Linnet. You do not need to feel shy.'

Linnet coloured. 'Thank you—but compared to this gathering I have done very little!' She glanced down the list. 'Who is Antonia Danieli?'

'Antonia is . . . Antonia,' Dina replied cryptically. She did not need to say any more.

During the afternoon before the dinner party, Max came into the dining-room and found Linnet kneeling on the floor, surrounded by flowers, great baskets full of roses and carnations and long-stemmed lilies, huge bunches of ferns and other greenery, chunks of oasis, bundles of chicken wire, and an assortment of vases, candlesticks and ornaments of all kinds.

He stopped short, looking over this scene of chaos with an expression of some trepidation.

'I trust you know what you are doing?' he said dubiously.

'Absolutely,' Linnet replied firmly, hoping the results would justify the confidence she was intent on displaying.

He did not look too convinced.

'I could always have hired someone for the job, but then Aunt Dina would have been really hurt,' he said. 'I'm only surprised she has relinquished it so completely to you.'

'She trusts me, unlike some I could mention,' Linnet said, and it occurred to her that he obviously didn't care a hoot if his doubting manner hurt *her* feelings. 'There is no need for you to worry. I've done dozens of these things. In fact,' she added flippantly, 'if my voice doesn't come back, I can always get a job as a florist.'

His response to this was swift and alarming.

'Don't say that—don't even allow yourself to think it!' he reprimanded her.

Linnet looked up at him, her face set, her eyes wide and direct. 'Why not? It would be all the same to you, Max,' she said calmly.

A look of what she could only describe as disgust swept across his face, darkening his brow and curling his upper lip.

'Sometimes, Linnet, I think you have a mental age on a par with Cosima's,' he said witheringly. 'No wonder you two get on so well together!'

With that he turned and stalked out of the room, irritation expressed in every line of his erect back and straight shoulders. Linnet gazed after him thoughtfully. She should have been offended, but, oddly, her predominant emotion at that moment was a niggardly satisfaction. She had rattled him—upset his infernal composure. She did not know why that pleased her, unless it was a low desire to return hurt for hurt. No doubt it was an unworthy sentiment, but none the less she felt better for it.

The pleasure she derived from her completed handiwork was far more wholesome. Dina clapped her hands in delight at the sight of the table, with individual posy vases beside each place-setting complementing the central arrangement. As a final touch, Linnet had twined ferns and tuberoses artfully around the branches of the chandelier, and could hardly wait for it to be dark enough to switch on the lamps and display the full, glorious effect.

'*Bella—bellissima*—Linnet, you are much cleverer at this than I am!' Dina exclaimed generously. 'Go now and give yourself time to rest before you must get ready.' She sighed. 'There has not been much entertaining this year—you will understand why.'

'Of course,' Linnet said swiftly. 'A death in the family...' She had a quick mental picture of Joanna, seated at one end of this vast table, presiding graciously as hostess, but it was just as quickly erased by Dina, who said,

'In fact it is some time since Max had business colleagues home to dinner. In recent years he has entertained them in restaurants. Joanna liked only parties, you see... with her own friends. This kind of thing did not amuse her.'

Nor do I expect it to amuse me, Linnet thought drily, but Joanna would not have been overawed. Just bored?

But Max was her husband, and entertaining his associates was surely one of the duties the wife of such a man was expected to perform.

'But didn't Max...? I mean, I would have thought he would insist...' Linnet floundered, thrown by the notion of the autocratic Max di Angeli being driven from his own home.

'To begin, *si*.' Dina shrugged. 'But important business needs a...a good atmosphere, you would say?'

Linnet had to agree. More cracks, she thought perplexedly. Each time she turned her scrutiny on the fairy-tale marriage, yet another flaw appeared. And not a few of them, so it would seem, had been caused by Joanna. But all that long afternoon she had spent with Linnet, roundly slating and condemning her husband in terms so harsh as to be vitriolic, she had never once admitted, for even a split second, that she might herself have contributed to the problems within the marriage.

And for all Linnet tried hard to excuse her friend, to argue that Joanna, distraught and drinking heavily, had scarcely known what she was saying that afternoon, she could not hold back the ever-multiplying doubts. Could it be that Max the villain was, at least in part, Max the victim? *Max*? It was too hard to swallow! Linnet shook her head despairingly as she went slowly up to her room to change.

Looking around at the little group assembled for drinks before dinner, Linnet was glad she had forced herself to be extravagant and buy the lace suit after all. The room was awash with the very latest in fashion. Far from being staid and conservative, the middle-aged businessmen's wives were both stylish and glamorous. Cousin Arturo's blonde, aquiline consort looked like a princess and probably was one, Linnet thought. The men were all urbane and groomed, the conversation was witty, intelligent and conducted, as Dina had predicted, mostly in English, but from what she heard from time to time Linnet realised that these European magnates could slip back and forth through half a dozen languages without difficulty.

Arturo de Reyes had brought along his daughter, a fair, long-legged shy girl of about eighteen, whose eyes kept darting adoringly towards Max, and something clicked in Linnet's mind.

'That can't be Antonia?' she whispered to Dina.

'No, that's Trini,' Dina replied. 'I'll introduce you. She and Max are second or third cousins, I forget which. She's very young, but impeccably brought up, and a sweet child. There might just be a possibility...'

She couldn't really mean... Linnet thought incredulously... In this day and age, marriages were just not dreamed up that way... But after a few minutes' chat with the shy Spanish girl she knew she was not too far off the mark. It was obvious from the way Cousin Max kept creeping into the conversation, the way her eyes followed him all the while, that Trini would not be averse.

Clearly, he would have no trouble with her, Linnet thought. She adored him and would know her place. But she seemed too quiet and fragile to hold such a man. Apart from her cousin Max, Trini loved horses and the countryside, it seemed. How would she cope in the golden cage of the Ca' Favorita? Max could break her heart all too easily, if he wanted to. But maybe he would be a kind and indulgent husband to a shy young wife?

And then Linnet noticed that Trini was not really concentrating on what she was saying. She was staring over

Linnet's shoulder, her gaze admiring and regretful at the same time, and Linnet half turned to discover the object of her fascination.

'Antonia!' Trini breathed, on a note of resignation. 'Oh—she just looks so beautiful!'

And so she did, dressed in a plain, shimmery silver sheath of a dress with leg-of-mutton sleeves, full to the elbow then tight to the wrist, her ebony hair a long, shining fall over one shoulder, emphasising the high, sculptured cheekbones and slanted golden eyes, her enigmatic smile savouring her grand entrance, rejoicing in her own certainty that she made every other woman in the room mediocre by comparison. It was the girl Linnet had seen with Max in Harry's Bar, on her very first day in Venice.

Trini might be 'suitable'. She might be distant kin, and more obviously acceptable. But Linnet sensed her air of defeat, her knowledge that she could not compete with this stunning Italian girl who even now had her hands in Max's, and her face upturned for his kiss. If this was her opposition, Trini had probably lost, and sadness was written on her pretty young face.

You and me both, kid, Linnet thought, and was suddenly and unbelievably devastated by the cold, fierce wind of emotion that swept over her, so much so that she had to turn away and pretend to be involved in choosing a canapé from a tray that one of the maids was handing round.

Her fingers shook, her breath was stifled somewhere in her chest, and she looked down, blinking away the stinging sensation in her eyes. She had seen this coming. Oh, yes, of course she had; she had seen it coming and looked away, with all the stubborn stupidity of a mesmerised rabbit unable to run from the roar and lights of an oncoming locomotive. But she had denied it, forbidden it, and refused to call it by its name until now, when she could no longer find anywhere to hide. Until now, when she saw him holding Antonia's hands and realised that what Dina had hinted was the truth—Max was a deeply eligible man who would sooner or later love and marry someone else.

And she could not bear it. *Because she loved him*. It was that simple. It was that terrible.

'Trini—how nice to see you again, *cara*! And how sweet you're looking!'

The throaty, seductive voice was right beside her, and Linnet half choked on a piece of smoked salmon as she watched the two girls embrace, Trini as wooden as a puppet, Antonia full of queenly confidence, as well she might be.

The amber eyes rested speculatively on Linnet for a second. 'Now where have we met before, I wonder?' she queried, her voice a softly dangerous purr. 'I thought I knew all Max's family and friends.'

'We haven't exactly met, but I saw you in Harry's Bar, some time ago,' Linnet said, unable to suppress the suspicion that she was being looked over and judged, that Antonia was annoyed at being unable to place her, and did not care for unknown elements in Max's life.

'Ah, yes—you are the one who is looking after Max's little girl. I did not at first recognise you.' Her eyes flickered over Linnet's clothes, mentally counting up what they had cost. 'I do like your suit—you must tell me who is the designer.'

Linnet told her. The designer was a new, up-and-coming young Italian, and she could almost see Antonia working out how Linnet had afforded such an outfit.

'Ah. Max is such a generous man,' she finally said, very softly.

'I'm sure he is,' Linnet said, a little stiffly. She had bought the suit herself, in the end, refusing to tell him where, but she was sure it would be only a matter of time before he found out.

'It's a legitimate business expense, Linnet,' he had said reasonably, but with a touch of impatience, earlier that evening. 'Why are you being so foolish?'

'I don't know, Max. Put it down to my retarded mental age,' she had retorted, and had been surprised to see a twinkle of appreciation chase the annoyance from his eyes. But there was nothing more she could do to squash Antonia's natural assumption that Max had picked up the bill, and all she wanted now was to get away from this beautiful, sharp-witted young woman whose birth, background and looks put her in line for the man Linnet loved.

It was almost a relief to stand and listen patiently, making sympathetic noises, as Gräfin von Rudesdorf told her a long story about how their plane had been delayed in New York. Antonia soon tired of this, and eased herself away, and as the talk ebbed and flowed Linnet was able to slip into the dining-room to check that everything was in order.

'It's perfect. When the job is done, and you know it was done well, forget about it,' said Max's voice behind her. He was leaning against the door-frame, looking suave and elegant in his dinner-suit with the black satin cummerbund and pin-tucked white shirt.

A pain started to spread from below Linnet's ribs—a deep nervous spasm that she recognised as the sensation which had afflicted her prior to singing before an audience. But then she would sing, and at that moment the pain would leave her, joy and confidence would flood in, and she would know all would be well.

But not now. This pain was caused by love, and she knew there was no remedy, and all would not be well. He was the man over whom Joanna had destroyed herself, the man Antonia was waiting eagerly to snare, and, however Linnet looked at it, he was not for her. Not now, nor ever.

She took a deep, calming breath and tried to look, speak and behave normally.

'You're right, I suppose.'

'I know I am. And thank you, Linnet, for all your hard work.'

'*Prego*,' she said automatically.

He smiled faintly.

'It *has* helped. Aunt Dina looks much more relieved,' he said, and Linnet's gaze followed his, through the open doorway, across the room to where Dina was laughing with Werner Passewald. The Swiss banker, a big, blond man in his fifties, had a hand on Dina's shoulder, and she was smiling up into his face. She looked, briefly, like a young girl.

'She's positively radiant!' Linnet exclaimed. 'Anyone would think that she . . .' She stopped herself swiftly, but Max looked down at her enigmatically, the corners of his mouth lifting slightly.

'That she was fond of him? Was that what you were about to say? Well, of course she is, Linnet. Old Werner has been after her since my uncle died, and they would be ideal for one another.'

Linnet, remembering what Dina had said about loneliness, murmured, 'Then why doesn't she marry him? What is she waiting for?'

'What do you think? She hasn't married him because she feels her responsibilities are here. She has held my family life together for years, and she won't put her own desires first until she's sure my life is in order. She's waiting, in short, for me to re-marry—to give Cosima a mother, and this home a heart.'

He looked down into her eyes with a grave sobriety that was a million miles from the casual, laughing playboy image he could assume so easily as and when it suited him. Linnet felt that she was being slowly strangled, her breath coming laboriously and with great difficulty through an aperture too narrow for it.

'And do you...do you think you will do that...soon?' she asked faintly.

'I expect so, songbird,' he said quietly, resignedly. 'I expect I shall.'

CHAPTER SEVEN

IT CAME as no surprise to Linnet that in his country house, as at the Ca' Favorita, Max had a room set aside where he dealt, from home, with matters related to his various businesses and the unpaid committee work he willingly undertook on behalf of the restoration of Venice.

What did surprise her was the ever-increasing amount of time he spent in there, sometimes emerging only in time for dinner, and returning to devote several hours more afterwards.

'You will give yourself an ulcer, or a heart attack,' she observed gravely one evening, watching him frown as he ran a hand through the sleekly waving dark hair.

'It's good of you to worry about my health, but had I wanted a nurse I would have employed one,' he said sardonically. 'Really, one cannot win with you, Linnet. You have taken me to task on more than one occasion for being away from home too often. So I try to be here—Cosima sees me every day—and still it's not enough.'

Linnet felt her cheeks grow warm. Had he truly taken so much notice of her admonitions, taken them to heart and acted on them? She could not have hoped for so much, and yet, deep down, she still dared not entirely trust his motives. Was he here because of what she had said, and for Cassie's sake? Or was he spending less time away because of Antonia? Was it true that he was seriously considering re-marriage?

It was pointless to torment herself with this question. She was now halfway through her contracted time in his employment. Once, it had stretched before her, as interminable as an eternity, a sentence she longed to end. Now, already, she had begun to dread the day when she must leave, convinced that when she did she would never see him again. Cassie was fond of her, but at her age, and with the rapidly approaching excitement of school and new friends, she would soon forget her. As for Max himself, he would most likely never give her another thought once she walked out of his house.

'Your trouble, Max, is that it's either one extreme or another,' she retorted a little tartly, and he gave that lazy grin that turned her heart over.

'Not at all. Tomorrow afternoon, I'm playing polo, so you see, I do have some recreation,' he said smugly. 'Is that all right by you? Not so long ago you were accusing me of having rather too much. You're almost as bad as Alba used to be.'

The warmth was now a stinging heat which threatened to betray the depth of her feelings.

'Concern for others is not unnatural,' she said stiffly.

'It's rarely unconditional, or without strings,' he said, a hint of regret beneath the cynicism. 'Alba loved me, I know, but she had two daughters of her own. Rightly, she must have loved them more, and I was always jealous. My father loved only business and my mother's memory. I doubt that he cared for me, other than as an heir to the tradition he'd inherited and the fortune he'd helped build. As for my dear wife——'

He stopped abruptly, on the verge of a revelation, and his mouth tightened firmly. Linnet saw bitterness and a shameful anger in his eyes, and her own breath constricted fiercely. What? she wanted to scream. Don't stop there—tell me!

But he said no more, and it was obvious he did not intend to. He had corrected his momentary slip in mid-flight, and once again his marriage was a closed and closely guarded subject.

'I can't accept that view of the world, or of the feelings of others,' Linnet said stoutly. 'Nor should you, when Cassie loves you and asks for nothing but your love in return. And Dina, by your own admission, has set aside her own dreams and desires on your behalf.'

He cast her a sidelong glance of great complexity.

'You're in full throttle today, songbird,' he said acidly. 'And speaking with all the wisdom of inexperience, yet to be disappointed.'

'How can you say I've never had a set-back in my life?' she exclaimed resentfully. 'If that were so, I wouldn't be here.'

'Ah, yes, but not one administered by another human being,' he pointed out. 'You are young, you'll recover, and sing again. And probably meet some young tenor, in the concert halls of the world, and get married into the bargain.'

The very fact of his speaking so calmly and casually of her future with someone else brought a sour taste to her mouth. It didn't matter to him, of course it didn't, so he could say such things lightly and without taking the subject too seriously. He didn't know, thank heaven, that she was sitting there with her heart aching for the need of him.

'I haven't even thought about it,' she said, and he gave a half-contemptuous laugh.

'*Cierto*, you have! Every woman thinks about it, from the age of thirteen or so!' he contradicted scornfully.

'They enter a room and at once cast their eyes around them for the best prospect! It's the way they are programmed. Twenty years on, they start doing the same thing for their daughters!'

'That might be the way Italian high society goes about it. Ordinary English girls usually wait until they meet someone and—and fall in love.'

Her hesitation over the last few words was fractional, but his raised eyebrows informed her that he had picked it up.

'And if, ruled entirely by their immature emotions, they have fallen for the wrong person?' he queried. 'If, led only by their hearts, they have chosen wrongly, and are unhappy?'

Linnet had the feeling, so strong as to be inescapable, that this conversation had ceased to be hypothetical, that they were no longer discussing an imaginary marriage, but his own.

'It's sad, and unfortunate, but not the end of the world,' she pointed out. 'People make mistakes, and sometimes they leave one another, but it doesn't mean they can't learn to love again.'

He shook his head.

'We look at it differently here,' he said. 'Marriage and the family come first, and are not to be so easily broken up by scandal or divorce. You make your bed, you lie on it, happy or not happy.'

'And no one ever has affairs or falls in love with someone else?' Linnet protested. 'I find that hard to believe.'

'It happens, but affairs are conducted with more discretion—especially by women,' he said. 'They aren't allowed to destroy the unity of the family. In effect, in the kind of family I belong to, love and marriage may well be entirely separate issues.'

Linnet shuddered.

'I couldn't marry without love,' she said emphatically.

He smiled, with a soft mockery which she sensed was directed entirely at himself.

'I used to think that, when I was young and enamoured of Anglo-Saxon morality,' he said. 'Now I have come to believe ours is the better way—without romantic expectations, with both eyes open, and a premarital contract drawn up by a good lawyer. That way, there's no room for error.' He glanced at the clock. 'And now, since you have delayed me here talking nonsense for the last half-hour, I shall have to work even later to compensate! I hope your conscience troubles you!'

Linnet sat on the darkening terrace long after he left, and her conscience *did* trouble her, but for reasons he could not have guessed. It troubled her because she had prejudged him before they had even met, and had continued to do so for some time, even against the mounting evidence of her own ears and eyes. He was no saint, and did not pretend to be, but neither was he the devil incarnate. The profligate pleasure-seeker of her imagination had turned out to be a hard-working individual with a fierce sense of family commitment, whose crime—if one could call it that—had been to marry a woman with whom he was deeply incompatible.

It was true that he indulged in life's enjoyments as voraciously as he gave himself to business. It was also undeniable that he had a keen Italian appreciation of women. But was it true that he had mistreated and cheated on his wife?

I shall probably never know for sure, Linnet told herself soberly. But in her heart she had begun to doubt and to wonder. How much of Joanna's ravings had been lies, how much sheer hysteria, and how much suppressed guilt for her own share in the failure of her marriage?

Linnet could not deny that she had been physically drawn to Max from the beginning, when she had still been convinced of his perfidy. That attraction had been spontaneous and outside the bounds of reason, a mysterious chemistry that paid no attention to right or wrong. But the love she felt for him now must have grown almost without her being aware of it, until it had hit her like a thunderclap on the night of the dinner party. It had matured silently, stealthily, as she had grown to know him better, faults, failings, good points and bad, as a human being. As a *man*. Could she have fallen in love with the man she had first believed him to be? Inexperienced she might be, but she was not a fool.

It's all academic, she thought wearily, getting up and closing the terrace doors softly behind her. She loved him, but meant nothing to him. He would marry again—someone suitable this time, 'without romantic expectations, with both eyes open.' Cassie would have brothers and sisters to play with on the beach, the Ca' Favorita would come to life with dinners and soirées, elegantly organised by a beautiful hostess. Dina would pick up her own life again and marry her Swiss banker. Happy ever after.

And me? she thought sadly. Well, she had merely strayed on to this set by mistake, and had no part in the scene. The cage door was open, and the bars had been an illusion all along. The bird was free to fly, but unfortunately her wings were badly scorched.

* * *

September in Italy was a beautiful month. It had always been Linnet's favourite time of year back home, maybe because her birthday fell during its final week. She had loved the misty mornings and the hints of gold and copper in the trees whose leaves would soon be starting to fall.

Here, the skies were still clear and blue every day, and at midday the heat could be strong. But, that apart, there was a gentler, mellower feel to the warmth, which was less enervating. In this cooler season, they returned to the Ca' Favorita. In Venice, she found that, although there were still plenty of visitors about, some of the frenzy had gone from the atmosphere, and it was a pleasanter city in which to wander.

A parcel from home arrived for Linnet a few days before her birthday, and set in motion a train of events which would not otherwise have occurred, since she had not intended mentioning the anniversary. But Cassie was there when the package was delivered, and squealed with eager anticipation, demanding it be opened immediately.

Her parents had sent her a beautifully illustrated book about the lives and work of several great operatic singers. Cassie leafed through it eagerly, exclaiming over the gorgeous costumes and stage sets.

'It's like Carnival week in Venice!' she declared. 'Is that what you did, Linnet, before you came to live with us?'

'Well, no—these are big stars, who are already famous,' Linnet explained. 'But one day, perhaps, I will.'

Cassie looked crestfallen.

'But then you would have to leave us! I don't want you to go!'

Linnet was deeply touched. '*Bambina*, you know I can't stay here forever,' she said gently.

'Why not?' Cassie's chin was mutinous, and for a moment she looked so much like Joanna, when she wanted her own way, that Linnet's heart twisted. 'Papà won't mind, I know! We must ask him.'

Papà would certainly mind, Linnet thought, horrified, and desperate to dissuade Cassie from taking any such action. She could not explain to this small, determined, lovable child that one day, in the not too distant future, she would have a new *mamma* to look after her, so she said, 'I don't think we should do that, Cassie. Your *papà* knows I must go back to my music, but perhaps one day he might take you to hear me sing.'

Cassie clapped her hands enthusiastically, distracted by this prospect, and then her sharp eyes spotted the birthday card half hidden under the wrapping paper which had covered the book.

'Ooh—Linnet, it's your birthday!' she cried. 'Is it today?'

'No, it's on Saturday,' Linnet admitted. 'I expect *my mamma* and *papà* wanted to be sure I got my present in good time. But Cassie, when you are twenty-two, you don't make a great fuss over birthdays. I mean, you don't have jelly and paper hats, and pass the parcel.'

Cassie was regarding her with a puzzled expression on her small face, as if she had never heard of such things, and an awful suspicion began to dawn on Linnet that this child had never had a proper children's party.

'What do you do on your birthday?' she asked.

Cassie thought hard.

'Papà takes me out to tea. Somewhere very grand——' she began, but just then Dina walked in, and she forgot what she had been about to say. 'Aunty Dina, Aunty Dina, it's Linnet's birthday on Saturday!' she announced importantly.

Dina smiled, and looked from the excited child to Linnet.

'Is it really? I expect you were going to keep very quiet about that, weren't you?' she said shrewdly. 'It is naughty of you, Linnet. We must celebrate, no? I will tell Aldo to prepare a special dinner.'

Linnet sighed and protested, 'Really, you must not go to any trouble——' But, seeing Dina's no-nonsense expression, she knew that argument would cut no ice, and suddenly an idea came to her.

'No—don't do that. Let's have a party, just ourselves. Jelly and cake and bananas in custard, and paper hats and streamers——'

'And pass the parcel?' Cassie interpolated.

'Of course,' Linnet promised solemnly.

Cassie jumped up and down gleefully. 'Papà must come!' she declared, and Linnet immediately began to doubt the wisdom of her impulsive decision.

'Oh . . . I don't know, Cassie. He may be too busy, and too grown up for such a thing.'

'You and Aunty Dina are not too grown up, so why should he be?' Cassie demanded logically, and there was no stopping her asking her father the minute she saw him at lunch the same day.

Max looked at Linnet over his daughter's head, and a gravely amused smile twitched at the corners of his mouth.

'This is your idea?'

'Sort of.' Linnet squirmed. She could hardly accuse him of depriving his own child of a pleasure she had imagined universal. And what could Joanna have been thinking of? Surely they had had children's parties at Verne Hall?

But, 'Papà takes me out to tea,' Cassie had said. Not Mamma, or both of them. What kind of a mother had Joanna been? Linnet wondered, appalled by her sudden, treacherous anger towards her friend. Had Cassie really known her at all?

'I think,' Max said, barely concealed amusement still flickering in his eyes, 'you had better confer with Aldo. He may not be acquainted with the mysteries of bananas in custard!'

'I'll arrange it all myself. I don't want to cause any bother,' Linnet said quickly.

'Linnet, my staff are paid to work, and "bother" is not a word in their vocabulary,' he said patiently, but in a manner that somehow reduced her to the size of Cassie. 'A little instruction and co-operation may be necessary, that is all. I am sure everyone will rise magnificently to the occasion.'

It was not possible to back down now, in the face of Cassie's enthusiasm, so Linnet was obliged to carry through what she had so innocently started. She scoured the back-streets of Venice in search of crêpe paper to make hats and streamers, haunted the stalls along the Riva degli Schiavoni for little novelties for the parcel.

And, as Max had hinted, the household entered into the spirit of the occasion as if they knew all too well that Linnet had devised all this for Cassie rather than for herself. She sensed a great outflowing of warmth towards her from all of them, a wonderful feeling of being not simply a member of staff in a great house, but part of a family, all bent towards the same end.

Signora Marchetti and the maids, giggling with childish delight, helped Linnet decorate the dining-room, festooning it with streamers and balloons, the table groaned with buns, jellies, biscuits, tiny sandwiches and sausages on sticks, and each plate had a paper hat and a small, carefully wrapped present beside it. Dina had unobtrusively disappeared—Linnet did not know where—but by seven o'clock, so as not to be too late for Cassie, everything was in readiness.

'Lovely!' she exclaimed, pleased with the production in spite of herself. '*Favoloso*!'

'*Molto favoloso*!' Signora Marchetti agreed, nodding happily, and they all collapsed into fits of giggles again, just as Max walked in.

Linnet straightened up and tried to put on a sober face, but her cheeks were flushed pink with enjoyment, and she was afraid, as ever, that he would be quite unable to take her seriously. But why should he? He had gone along with this only to please Cassie, who pranced into the room behind him, clutching a parcel almost as big as herself.

'For you!' she declared, thrusting it at Linnet.

'Well, go ahead. Open it,' Max ordered, and she didn't know whether his half-humorous expression was mocking or indulgent. He looked so unfairly handsome in his casual but beautifully cut beige suit which emphasised the tanned skin, the night-black hair, and the unbelievable blue of his eyes, that Linnet had to look away quickly, afraid that she might betray her own longings. She dropped to her knees, fumbling swiftly with the ribbons and wrapping paper, hoping that a flurry of preoccupied activity would mask the way she felt.

But her cry of surprise was genuine when the paper fell away and revealed a large Paddington Bear, correctly dressed to the last detail, exactly as in the latest book she had been reading to Cassie, who was now obsessed with Paddington and all his doings.

'Isn't he lovely? Do you like him?'

'He's gorgeous,' Linnet assured her. 'He shall sit at the end of my bed every night!' And in her spontaneous delight she could not help but look up at Max, to be utterly astounded by what she read in his eyes.

They had all dressed up—Cassie had demanded it, since this was a party—and Linnet was wearing a soft cream dress with a cross-over bodice which revealed her throat and defined the soft swell of her breasts, while the skirt flared out around her. Since the dinner party, she had discovered in herself a guilty liking for good clothes, and had spent some more of her generous salary in the boutiques of Venice. The material of the dress was whisper-soft, like a caress on her skin, and her hair, lightened yet further by the long weeks of sunshine, was caught behind her ears with gold clips and allowed to fall in a sleek swath over her shoulders. She could not herself know how the pleasure of the occasion had brought a warm sparkle to her grey eyes, and a honey glow to her skin, but on the face of the man looking down at her she was sure she saw a quickening of desire, a look which told her he thought her beautiful... and would like to tell her so by means other than words.

She gulped, swallowed, unable to cope with the sudden frightening onslaught of unknown sensations, and bent quickly to gather up the discarded paper.

'Lucky old Paddington,' he whispered mischievously in her ear, and then more loudly, for all to hear, 'He was hard to track down, Linnet. Luckily, I have my contacts.'

The mere thought of Max di Angeli sitting behind the desk in his office, phoning all around his business associates in search of a king-sized Paddington Bear, rescued Linnet from the terrifying seriousness of her own emotions, and she burst out laughing.

At that precise moment, Dina's mysterious absence was explained as she bustled in, followed by Aldo, who was bearing a huge cake, decoratively iced and bearing, in English and in Italian, the words 'Happy Birthday, Linnet', complete with twenty-two candles.

This was a complete surprise to Linnet, and her eyes filled with sudden tears. Blinking furiously, she exclaimed, 'Oh, no—it's too much!' and, seizing a paper napkin, she mopped them away furiously. Everyone was laughing, but affectionately, and she simply dared not look at Max.

'This is supposed to be a joyful occasion,' she heard him say drily. 'But if you think I am going to drink your health in fizzy orange you're very much mistaken, young lady!'

He clapped his hands, and in came Gianni, bearing a tray of glasses and bottles of vintage champagne. Corks popped, and everyone, all the staff included, had a full glass in his or her hand. Even Cassie had a little, well topped up with orange.

Max was holding out a glass for her, and there was no way Linnet could avoid his eyes while taking it. He was smiling faintly, now, and that deeply appreciative, savouring expression was replaced by a kind of gravity.

'To you, songbird,' he said quietly. 'May you long remember your Venetian birthday.'

As if she could ever forget it, Linnet thought, torn between happiness and despair. This day would live in her memory for years to come, the only birthday she would ever spend with the man she loved. She bit her lip hard, knowing that she must appear unreservedly glad, and not reveal the ambiguity of her feelings.

'Thank you—thank you all,' she said, smiling around. '*Grazie—molto grazie*!'

It was not the end. There were small gifts from each member of the staff, and Dina gave her an exquisite figurine of a bird in flight, lovingly designed in glass and executed as only a local craftsman could do. Candles were lit on the cake, and she was obliged to blow them out. As the flames flickered briefly and the smoke spiralled upwards, Max drew from his pocket a slim velvet box which he placed in Linnet's astonished hands.

'But you shouldn't... I have my Paddington, and the lovely bird——' she stammered.

'Those are from Cosima and Dina. This is from me,' he insisted. 'Open the box and please don't argue, Linnet. It's most ungracious.'

His reproof was gentle but very firm, and with nervous hands she did as she was bidden. On a bed of white silk lay a single strand of perfect, milky pearls, too fine to be anything but real, and she gasped aloud, 'I can't——'

'Don't be silly. It's a birthday gift, that's all,' he said equably, and, taking it from the box, he fastened it deftly around her neck. His fingers brushed the nape of her neck as he lifted her hair to close the diamond-studded clasp, and she felt her whole body flood with an excess of unbearable warmth, followed instantly by an icy shivering.

She knew this feeling now. She wanted him—his arms around her, the tingling contact of his body with hers, his kiss—the way he had kissed her long ago, in the study. If he were to kiss her like that again, there was no way she could prevent herself from responding... and from wanting more. As he moved away from her, she almost swayed under the power of her own sensual longing. She felt she could not bear it if he did not touch her again.

Linnet shook herself abruptly. This was a party, there were other people present, including a young child. She should not be thinking like this.

'It's a beautiful necklace, Max,' she said. 'You should not have bought it for me...but since you have...thank you very much.'

'I buy what I want, for whom I want.' He shrugged negligently. 'And since you foolishly refused to let me pay for that dress you were obliged to buy for the dinner party——'

Linnet turned away, suddenly sick at heart, glad he was speaking so softly that no one else had heard. The pearls were not a gift, they were a payment, that was all. He had found a way, in spite of her refusal, to recompense her for what she had spent on the dress. And after all, what was the money to him? He could so easily afford this nonchalant generosity. What mattered to him was being in control, and proving it, doing what *he* wanted to do, no matter if the needs and feelings of others ran contrary to this primary urge to mastery.

For over an hour, Linnet doled out jelly and sandwiches, cut her cake and played party games, striving bravely to keep up the party atmosphere everyone else was so effortlessly enjoying. But the simple pleasure she had been overflowing with earlier had evaporated for her, and it was no more than a masquerade.

When at last it was all over, the staff were busy clearing up, Cassie had gone happily to bed, and Dina had retired to her room, declaring that she was replete and exhausted, Linnet's shoulders drooped a little, less from any real fatigue than from the strain of maintaining the pretence.

'I think I shall go to my room as well, Max,' she said quietly.

He blocked her as she moved towards the door.

'Not yet,' he said mysteriously. 'It is still your birthday, and besides it's far too early. Come with me.'

'But Max——' She sighed, anxious only to get away from him now, to be alone with her sad sense of disillusionment. In reply, he took her arm firmly, and led her, still reluctant but too dispirited to protest further, through the dining-room and along the hall to the front door of the *palazzo*, where Gianni, a conspiratorial smile on his face, was waiting to open it.

Outside, the sky was darkening and a full moon rising, making pathways of glimmering light across the gently splashing waters, and drawn up against the water-gate Linnet saw the unmistakably high prow and curved, elegant shape of a gondola, with the gondolier standing still, resting at ease on his oar.

'What——?' she began, puzzled, but he was already guiding her into the craft.

'I know—I've heard all the arguments. Gondolas are expensive, they are a tourist cliché, the Venetians travel everywhere by *vaporetto*. But just once, Linnet, this is an experience you should have.'

The craft rocked gently on the water, and Linnet, still bemused, had no choice but to comply as Max drew her down beside him on the padded seat. This was not just any passing gondola. They reclined beneath a covered canopy, and in front of them, on a small table, was champagne resting in a bucket of ice, and two crystal goblets. Max signalled to the gondolier, who turned his back on them and pushed the boat off, into the centre of the canal.

'Hackneyed, isn't it?' said Max, his sardonic smile very white in the semi-darkness. 'Don't worry—I haven't paid him to serenade us, although I will, if you want me to.'

Linnet had known far too many different emotions that day than were good for her. She had been innocently happy, grateful, shaken by desire, and bitterly disappointed. And now here she was, gliding along, past lighted *palazzos* and café terraces full of people, with a brilliant moon above, and Max di Angeli by her side. She no longer knew whether it was joy or sorrow she was feeling; she was too dazed... it all seemed to be happening in a dream.

As they drifted along the Grand Canal towards the brilliantly lit Rialto, he expertly uncorked the champagne and filled the glasses.

'Oh... I think I've already had too much of this today,' she said dreamily, but she drank it all the same, and he laughed softly. His arm rested lightly around her shoulders, and falling under the spell of the champagne, the magic of Venice all around them, the thrill of him beside her, warm and vibrantly male, Linnet wished this might not end, that they might float along forever like this, just the two of them. No world beyond, no complications, no past or future.

The gondola turned off into a small, quiet canal, where tall, dark buildings and shadowy bridges blotted out the moonlight.

'Enough,' Max said, taking the glass from her hand and setting it on the table. 'I want you to be happy, Linnet, but not insensible. I want you to know what you're doing—what *I'm* doing.'

His arm tightened round her, his other hand lightly tipped back her chin, and his mouth closed on hers, stopping her breath, her thoughts, and filling her with an incredible sweetness. It went on and on, endlessly, and she knew she had been waiting for this for so long...longer than she dared admit. Her lips clung to his and parted, and she was drowning in him, unwilling to let go, innocence and sensuality fused into one.

It was he who finally freed her mouth, but only in order to trace the line of her throat with his lips.

'I've been waiting all day to do this,' he murmured, and Linnet's senses began to spin, less from the heady effect of the wine than from an irresistible, guilty craving for his touch. 'And this, too——' as his hands slipped easily inside the bodice of her dress to close around her breasts.

Linnet was afraid she would die, either from the pleasure his caress induced in her, or from the insatiable desire for more. Her whole body was tingling almost unbearably, but they were in a moving craft, under the open sky, with the broad back of the gondolier only feet in front of them.

'Oh, Max, don't——' she gasped. 'It's not right...I mean...in public...'

His gently knowing fingers continued to explore, knowingly, pleasingly.

'It's dark, Linnet, and besides far more than this happens in gondolas,' he said. 'But there's no need for you to be alarmed. I've no intention of making love to you here. This is just for starters. Then we'll go home.'

His stark, matter-of-fact assumption that he was free to make love to her as and when he chose, that her assent was already given, or could be taken for granted, startled her, clearing her head and bringing her back to her senses with a jolt. Pulling herself free of his caressing hands, she shrank back into her corner of the seat.

'You do this kind of thing—and more—in gondolas often, I suppose,' she said accusingly, a hot shame creeping up her neck, so that she was glad of the darkness. 'Lay on the bubbly, and tell the gondolier to find the darkest canals!'

He made no attempt to pull her back into his arms. Indeed, he did not touch her at all.

'Gondoliers don't need telling such things,' he said with mild scorn. 'What's the matter, Linnet? You were keen enough a moment ago, as I recall. You're free—I'm free. Is there any reason why we should not make love, if we both want to?'

Every reason! she wanted to exclaim bitterly. She was a woman in love, and he was simply giving in to a passing whim. Or maybe, she thought, mortified, he thought he would be giving her yet another birthday treat. A handsome, aristocratic lover she should be humbly grateful to have briefly in her bed!

'You assume too much, Max!' she cried angrily. 'You assumed I wanted to simply because *you* did. It always has to be your way, doesn't it? That's why you gave me the pearls, because I insisted on paying for the dress——'

'Forget about the damn dress!' he exclaimed, so furiously that she almost jumped. 'I bought you the pearls because it was your birthday and I wanted you to have them. I hired the gondola because I thought you would enjoy it. And I kissed you because I found you desirable. *It is that simple*! What sort of world do you come from, what sort of mind do you have, that you are always seeking devious motives, complications, payments for everything?

'Don't you ever accept anything freely, Linnet? And don't you ever give anything the same way?'

CHAPTER EIGHT

IF THE gondolier wondered why he was ordered to return directly to the Ca' Favorita, he did not pass any comment, merely turned his craft philosophically and did as he was asked.

He must have seen it all before, Linnet thought, galled. Love-affairs that started, or failed to start, as he rowed along, brief couplings or silent struggles going on, literally, behind his back. Venice was made for sexual intrigue. But *she* most definitely was not, Linnet decided ruefully. She lacked the sophistication to enjoy a swift affair with Max, for all she had wanted him. And she had—oh, she had!

After his outburst, he was deathly quiet as they glided back along the canals, and she could not tell if he was angry, disgusted, or just plain contemptuous. Not knowing was more than she could bear, and she tried to break the silence with some sort of explanation.

'Max—you don't understand. I'm not the kind of girl who casually—well, you know...'

'No, I don't know, Linnet,' he said coldly. 'I realise you are a virgin, but there is a first time for everyone, and the world no longer divides neatly into good girls who don't, and bad girls who do. Do you think I would have given you a bad experience? That I don't know what a woman needs, and how to treat her?'

'Oh, I'm sure you know that only too well!' she retorted, stung, and the light from a passing window briefly showed her his face, dark with suspicion.

'And what exactly is that supposed to mean?'

'Oh... nothing.' She pressed a hand wearily to her forehead. 'Can't we just go home and forget all about it? I'm very tired.'

'Certainly.' He shrugged. 'I'll be glad to do that. But if I might give you some advice, in words I actually learned from an English friend...? If you aren't going to make the tea, don't put the kettle on.'

Linnet half turned her back on him, furious, but there was no sensible denial she could make. She had gone willingly into his arms, she had been more than eager to be kissed and touched, and it did not require a lot of experience to know where all that would irrevocably lead.

She had let herself drift along, seduced by the romantic atmosphere, the wine and the moonlight, into a dream world where she loved him and he loved her, and that made it all right.

But he didn't love her. He desired her, and had decided, in his imperious way, that he would be her lover for tonight—maybe longer, if it suited him, but who knew? His sudden, practical matter-of-factness had shattered her romantic illusions. Without intending to—for to him it did not mean that much—he could break her heart. Remember that you will leave here one day soon, she warned herself. You will soon be forgotten, but you would not forget.

She would have refused his helping hand as the gondola drew up outside the Ca' Favorita, but a sudden wave caused the craft to rock alarmingly, and she was obliged to accept his assistance as she climbed out. But his hand did not linger under her elbow, and he walked apart from her as an impassive Gianni opened the door to admit them.

'There is no need to shrink away from me, Linnet,' he said, seeing she was about to hurry upstairs. 'Everything will remain precisely as it was. You work for me, and that is all. I shan't be groping you in dark corners, or making improper suggestions. That's not my style.'

'I... I never thought it was,' she said in a small, affronted voice.

'Then don't look so worried. You are perfectly safe.' He gave a world-weary sigh. 'Goodnight, songbird, and, once again, happy birthday.'

She watched him head off in the direction of his study before turning and slowly climbing the stairs to her room. Only with the door closed behind her did she dare to relive, in her memory, the events of the evening. The dark shadows under the bridges... his mouth exploring her neck and throat, making her shiver with excitement... A strong temptation seized her to run after him along the dimly lit corridors, to say, Here I am, take me. I don't want to be safe, I want to be yours. Even though I know you don't love me.

She resisted it with all the strength of her will, not now out of virtue or fear, but because she knew he would only laugh at her and send her on her way. She had had her chance and refused it, and he knew her for what she was—a scared, inexperienced girl. Not the kind of woman Max di Angeli could take seriously.

She carefully removed the pearls he had given her, and laid them on their bed of silk in the box which the maid must have put on her dressing-table. She could not insult this proud man by giving them back. 'I bought you the pearls because it was your birthday and I wanted you to have them,' he had said, and she knew that, whatever the motivation, they were not an exchange for favours he intended to collect. He had no need to operate that way. Women would come to him without any inducement save for his personal charm. She would keep the pearls. But she would never wear them again.

'It's just you and me, I guess, Paddington,' she said as she slipped into bed and pulled the quilt up to her chin. She wouldn't cry, she told herself firmly. There was no point. Some things in this world you could not have, and no amount of weeping would give them to you, or assuage the lack of them. For her, the love of Max di Angeli was just one of those things.

A few days passed, and suddenly, one morning, Max called Linnet into his study after breakfast. What have I done wrong now? was her automatic reaction, an instinctive flashback to her early days at the Ca' Favorita, when she had seemed to be forever putting her foot in it.

She told herself that it was plain stupid of her to think that way. It had been a long time since Max had been able seriously to find fault with her. She had a good relationship with Cassie, got on well with Dina, and, especially since the party, all the staff were friendly with her. It was difficult for her to see how and where she might have transgressed.

But she was uneasy, for since the night of the gondola ride there had been a marked difference in his manner towards her. He was always perfectly correct, but so icily formal that it did not seem possible that they had trembled briefly on the edge of becoming lovers. If it were not that she remembered so achingly the touch of his hands, she might have convinced herself that it had never happened.

At first she had thought he had simply been annoyed with himself for misjudging the ease with which she could be seduced—for having, this once, overestimated the power of the di Angeli charm. Then another, altogether more embarrassing suspicion had crept up on her. Perhaps he was regretting the impulse which had urged him to make love to a girl who was a nonentity in his life—a mere employee, after all. Perhaps his brief and quickly quenched desire had embarrassed him.

Whatever his reasoning, he had taken good care never to be alone with her, and she, on her part, had been equally careful to avoid him as much as she could. And so they met only at mealtimes or family occasions, and had no conversations which did not include a third party. Skirting around each other, Linnet thought, chastened, as she made her way to his study—until now, when this sudden summons meant she must once more face him alone.

He was seated behind his desk and a mountain of paperwork, his face its usual polite mask, virtually expressionless.

'Have a seat, Linnet,' he said. 'I won't keep you long.'

She slid nervously on to the edge of the chair.

'Is something wrong?' she asked.

'Wrong?' He looked blankly at her. 'No, of course not. Why should it be?' He sliced open a letter with a damascened paper-knife, obviously not of a mind to waste time, scanned the letter briefly, frowning at its contents, and returned his attention to her.

'It simply occurred to me that as we are now into October, you will soon be wanting to make plans for your future—after you leave here.'

Linnet suppressed a start of alarm. It sounded uncommonly as though he wanted to be rid of her. As though, as she had thought, she had become something of an embarrassment.

'Well . . . yes,' she replied slowly. 'Although as regards my training I cannot make any firm arrangements until I see the specialist in January, and, hopefully, he gives me the all-clear.'

'I realise that, and I too hope that the results are good for you,' he said punctiliously. 'But your contract with me will expire well before that, and I expect that, anyhow, you will want to be home in England for Christmas so that you can spend it with your family.'

'You are looking well ahead,' she said wryly, and suddenly words she had not planned to say came tumbling out of their own volition. 'You know—just because you—er—kissed me . . . there's no reason for you to worry that I'm likely to keep reminding you of it. As you said yourself, our relationship will continue to be . . . just as it was before.'

'Whatever that was,' Max said cryptically, with the suggestion of a smile. 'And you are reminding me right now, Linnet, in case you hadn't noticed.'

'Yes, but . . . I didn't mean to . . .' she said, flustered, aware that he had subtly wrong-footed her once again. 'But I won't. Not intentionally.'

'I'm really not worried about it, Linnet,' he said wearily. 'Do you honestly think I have nothing else to trouble my head over? It's simply that, as a businessman, I am used to thinking and planning things in advance. I merely wanted to remind you to do the same. That's all.'

He returned once more to opening his letters, dark head bent, and Linnet realised with a shock that she was dismissed. She got up, and stumbled from the room, numb and speechless.

The message he had summoned her there to deliver was painfully clear to her. She was a hired hand, under a contract which would shortly terminate. Don't imagine, he was telling her, that because one night he had decided to amuse himself with her the conditions of that contract had changed in any way, that it had given her any sort of privilege, or claim on him, or otherwise altered her status. It had not.

Nor would it have, Linnet realised painfully, if the events of that night had worked out differently, and she had ended up in his bed. He would still be the blue-blooded European patrician, and she would still be the paid help, no more. There was no way her position would have changed, or her significance in his life increased.

You had a narrow escape there, my girl, she told herself sternly. She should be relieved and glad that she had not given way to temptation.

So why, then, was she not feeling this wholly appropriate emotion? Why wouldn't her disobedient heart fall in line with the instructions her head was so clearly giving it?

'I don't know what's the matter with Max these days,' Dina said to her one afternoon as they drank tea in her small parlour. It was mid-October and there had been a sudden change in the weather. The temperature had dropped sharply, and a thick fog had swirled in from the lagoon, creeping sinuously round the feet of the ancient buildings and obscuring the views from the ground-floor windows. It was a foretaste of what winter would be like in Venice—a very different place from the hot, cloudless summer city.

'How do you mean?' Linnet was deliberately cautious. 'I. . . I haven't really seen an awful lot of him lately, so it would be difficult to say if anything were wrong.'

'Exactly so,' Dina pronounced. 'He keeps more to himself all the time, says little, thinks much. As if he has something very important, very serious on his mind.'

Linnet sipped her tea and replaced the cup carefully on its saucer before replying, 'I expect he has some big business deal which is preoccupying him.'

Dina shook her head.

'I don't think so. Business is going on all the time, it has been a part of his life for many years, and he is used to coping with it. I believe something more personal is involved.'

'Like... marriage?' The cold mist seemed to have insinuated its way indoors and wrapped itself around Linnet's heart.

'Perhaps.' Dina frowned. 'It would be good for him, of course, but it is not a decision he should rush to make. This time, he must choose the right girl, for the right reasons, and not be mistaken.'

'I don't suppose he thought he was making a mistake the first time, if he was in love,' Linnet said.

'You know nothing about it, Linnet, since you were not here at the time,' Dina said, rather sharply, for her. 'He had argued with his father, who had his own ideas about Max's future. My brother could be... well, the kind of person who always thought he knew best, and expected others to do as *he* wished.'

Like father, like son, Linnet thought wryly. She was sorely tempted to retort that she actually knew more about it than anyone realised, but... did she? It had been a nine-day wonder in the village. One minute, Joanna and Rupert had been inseparable, although their relationship was never official, and the next, out of the blue, she was going to marry some Italian aristocrat.

'Max went off to Paris in a terrible temper to attend a gala ball,' Dina continued. 'He came back engaged to marry an English girl none of us had ever met.'

Linnet dimly remembered Joanna going to Paris—but then, she had always been chasing off somewhere. And by then, she thought, with sudden painful clarity, she had come to see less and less of her childhood heroine. 'Not now, mouse, I'm busy,' she would say impatiently, if Linnet sought her out, and, although her loss of interest had hurt Linnet, the diffident girl she had then been readily made excuses for it—Joanna had lots to do, crowds of friends, was in great demand. Now, with the hindsight of steadily growing maturity, she realised that she had only really had Joanna's attention when it had amused the older girl to bestow it.

She had run eagerly up to the Hall when the news of the impending marriage reached her along the grapevine, and tracked Joanna down to the stables where she was grooming her hunter.

'Joanna, Joanna, you're getting married! Can I be a bridesmaid?' she had begged, beside herself with excitement.

Joanna had looked at her languidly over the horse's chestnut flank.

'You? Lord, no, mouse, I hardly think so,' she had said bluntly. 'For one thing the wedding is going to be in Italy. My gorgeous new fiancé absolutely insists on it, and I'm not going to argue! Besides, you're not family. And all the bridesmaids will be little girls.' She had looked disparagingly at Linnet, who at the time was thin and gawky, with bony wrists and ankles.

Of course, Joanna had lots of little cousins, and so, probably, had her fiancé, Linnet had reasoned, trailing disconsolately home. She wondered now where she had buried this unpleasant memory all these years. Perhaps she had conveniently forgotten it simply because it was hurtful.

'You're right—I wasn't there,' Linnet agreed, as lightly as she could. 'And I won't be here if and when he next gets married. I shall be back in England by Christmas.'

'We shall miss you,' Dina said. 'But it is natural—you have more to do with your life, no?'

Linnet only smiled and let her think it. It was better that way. Less than a year ago, she could not have envisaged a life without singing. Now she knew that even if her voice came back, allowing her to pick up where she had left off, music would no longer fill her life completely, as it once had. She had never dreamed, in those days, that she would find something else that was of equal importance. But then, in those days she had never loved a man. Now she did, and it was as if she had crossed a frontier which had closed behind her, and she could not go back. She was someone else now, and it was frightening.

Her own sombre thoughts and Dina's reflections about Max's future plans made it impossible for Linnet to rest easy, and after tea was finished she suddenly decided that she had to get out of the Ca' Favorita, if only for a little while. She shrugged into a short jacket that was not really warm enough for the change in the weather, but for all that she persisted in going out, slipping unseen through the back door.

There were few people about on this chilly afternoon, and Venice bore an uneasy resemblance to an empty stage set. Linnet's heels rang and echoed on the cobbles, the mists drifted and swirled around her, giving the occasional dimly seen passer-by a sinister, unreal appearance. Only the lighted bars and cafés spoke of life and people, but she was reluctant to go in, because she was alone and conspicuous. So she kept on walking, both to keep warm and to distract her mind. Neither objective was achieved. Her heart was still full of Max—Max who could not be hers, but would soon have someone else to fill his arms and his life. Max whom she had come here determined to hate, and who had somehow, without even trying, or caring, persuaded her to love him. And she was chilled to the bone as she slipped back indoors the way she had come.

'Linnet.'

His voice apprehended her, quiet but far from pleasant, and she turned, startled, to see him standing there, arms folded, regarding her with an expression on his face that turned her blood to ice, because she could not quite define it. If it was anger, then it was a cold, deathly anger, laced with contempt and a fathoms-deep disillusionment. It made her feel like something verminous which had crept from beneath a stone, which he was about to grind beneath his heel and destroy before it contaminated the entire household.

'Max...you made me jump. It's so cold out there, I really should buy a warmer coat...' she babbled stupidly, hearing herself and thinking how inane she sounded in her nervousness.

'Never mind that.' His voice was brusque and unconcerned with niceties. 'In my study—now.'

'But I——'

'I said *now*.' There was no escaping such implacability, and without another word Linnet preceded him down the corridor, aware of his heavy tread behind her, without a solitary clue to help her work out what this was all about, but unmistakably sure that it boded no good for her.

He closed the door behind her, but did not invite her to sit, nor did he take his own seat behind the desk. He simply pointed to a small wooden box on the desk-top.

'This is familiar to you, I presume?'

Linnet stared down at it, and a cold sensation spread uncomfortably down her back and into her legs, until she felt weak and in danger of imminent collapse. It was a musical box, very old, with a figure of a ballerina on the lid, and when opened, Linnet knew, the ballerina pirouetted around, and if the key underneath it had been wound it played Chopin's Minute Waltz.

She knew this because it had once stood on a table in Joanna's room at Verne Hall, where it had, in those days, held her diary—'the one with the things I don't want Mummy to read about,' she had smirked.

Linnet was frozen speechless, like a statue carved from ice. Her brain had stopped functioning and only her appalled senses were reacting furiously, sending shivers along her spine.

'Open it,' Max said grimly, and, when she did not immediately react, in a voice only slightly raised, but even more ominous, repeated, 'I said, open it. Go on.'

With nerveless fingers, Linnet opened the lid. The key was unwound, the ballerina did not dance, and the clockwork mechanism did not play the Minute Waltz, but inside was a mere handful of photos, and Linnet, mesmerised, could not prevent herself from picking them up, which was exactly what he wanted her to do.

Joanna. Joanna on her horse. Joanna standing beside her maroon MG on the day she had been given it—her eighteenth birthday. Joanna and Rupert at a hunt ball, she wearing a floaty white dress. Joanna in her school uniform.

Linnet lifted her eyes to Max's face, stunned by the hostility she encountered in the glacial blue eyes.

'As you see, I have finally been sorting through some of my late wife's *effects*,' he said, laying cool emphasis on the last word. 'She brought very little with her from her old home—but you would have gambled on that, I expect.'

'I——' Linnet began, half choked, but he cut her off briskly.

'In fact, this box is all I found, stuffed at the bottom of an old trunk, and in seven years of marriage I had never seen it before,' he said, icily controlled. 'Go on, Linnet—you haven't seen all the photographs yet. What's that one at the bottom? Ah, yes—the Verne Hall Guide troupe.'

Taking it from her unresisting hand, he turned it over and read what was written on the back, not in Joanna's careless scrawl, but in Lady Verne's neat, precise hand.

'Susie, Jane, Claire, Polly, Lissa, Tracey—and Linnet. *Linnet*?' His brow puckered with feigned puzzlement. 'There she is, you see, second from the end. She has changed quite a lot, wouldn't you say?' His eyes raked over her, and returned to the photograph. 'I just might not have recognised her without the names on the back. But—Linnet? Pollys and Janes may be a dozen to the *lira*, but there are not so many devious, scheming little songbirds around!'

Linnet's temporarily paralysed brain cells had begun to work again, frantically. So what she had initially feared had happened, and he had discovered her connection with Joanna. Over the months, this anxiety had faded, the possibility becoming ever less likely, but now he had found out, and as she had expected he was furious at having been deceived. But she had not expected anger and disgust of this magnitude. It had been a deception, yes, but not a crime.

She fought back the only way she could—by taking the offensive herself.

'All right, you don't have to carry on with the funny business. It's me in the photo,' she admitted briskly. 'So what? Don't you think you're over-reacting a little?'

He was not even remotely impressed by this argument.

'You think so?' he challenged. 'You have lived for several months in my house, more as a member of the family than a member of staff, and all that time you have deliberately concealed the fact that you knew my wife. And it wasn't a slight acquaintance, by the sound of it. You come from the same village. You visited her home. In fact, you knew—know—the Vernes very well, don't you, Linnet?'

She swallowed hard, her head went back defensively.

'I wanted the job. I thought you wouldn't give it to me if you knew.'

'Why shouldn't I?' he rapped sharply. 'What difference would it have made? Give me one sensible reason why I should have refused you simply because you knew my wife—given that you were honest about it? It doesn't add up, Linnet, and you know it.'

There was only one possible defence she could plead now—the simple truth. Taking a deep breath, she said, 'I came here nursing a grudge against you... thinking you were some kind of amoral monster. I wanted to find out what had really happened to you and Joanna. You might think that was monumental cheek, but... it's the truth.'

'And?' He was regarding her with the same slow, unforgiving stare.

'And . . . I found out it wasn't really that clear-cut at all,' she faltered. Her eyes sought his, sure that the honesty of her words must be written on her face, and that he must believe her, but from his stony expression she could see that he was quite unmoved, and her heart sank.

'Very good, Linnet. You think on your feet with remarkable agility, but it won't do,' he said curtly. 'I think you're lying.'

With sudden, dangerous stealth, he moved closer to her, and his hard fingers gripped her shoulders, causing her to flinch with pain.

'I know why you are here. Shall I tell you?' His voice was unpleasantly soft. 'You are here because Lady Verne sent you to spy on me—to find out how I live, and if I am a fit father for Cosima. I know, from certain things she said to me at the funeral, that if the Vernes could make a case for trying to get custody they would. Small wonder you don't need the salary I pay you—I expect they are reimbursing you handsomely themselves!'

Just for a moment, this accusation knocked the wind out of Linnet, so there was a split second's hesitation before she cried out indignantly, 'That's not true! You can ask Lady Verne yourself, if you won't believe my word for it!'

That brief pause before her denial had, she saw, only condemned her further in his eyes.

'And she would surely admit to it, naturally,' he said sarcastically. 'Come on, Linnet, she would abandon you without a qualm, so don't take me for a fool. I see now the reason for all those sly little queries about Joanna and me, all that prurient snooping into my private life! I'm very sorry if I failed to give you enough ammunition!'

He let her go abruptly, dropping his hands from her shoulders as if he feared the mere touch of her might defile him.

'It's not true!' she repeated urgently, desperate in her need to convince him. 'How can I make you believe me?'

'Believe you?' His voice was thick with incredulous scorn. 'I *believed* you were fond of Cosima. I *believed* you had developed some affection for this household and everyone in it. I always admired the English for the sense of fair play—my God, I should have learned otherwise by now!'

His shoulders rose and fell in a gesture of utter finality. 'I shall never again believe anything you choose to tell me, Linnet.'

She stared helplessly at him. His face was set into hard, unyielding lines, his mouth, which she had seen in all aspects—tender, amused, desirous—was now taut and harsh. She saw that there was nothing she could say or do which would persuade him of her innocence. Her deception had rebounded on her with truly horrendous results. The whole thing was beyond redemption.

She drew herself up, holding her head very high and straight, deciding that since he was determined to find her guilty she refused to plead or otherwise defend herself any further.

'I suppose you want me to leave,' she said quietly.

'No, I do not,' he contradicted sternly. 'For all I'm sure it would suit you now to scuttle back whence you came, you don't escape the consequences of your actions that lightly.'

He paused, snapping closed the lid of the musical box with surprising violence.

'I have carefully prepared Cosima for the fact that you will be leaving us by Christmas. I think you owe it to me...and, more importantly, to her...to abide by that schedule. So you'll stay, Linnet, until it suits me for you to leave. I might add that for me, as for you, that moment cannot arrive too soon.'

With that he turned his back on her, concluding the interview, but Linnet could not move. Mind, heart and body, she was still in shock that anyone could have spoken to her in such a way, or thought her capable of such duplicity. To have endured such treatment from the man she loved, to know that he despised her so thoroughly, froze her limbs and her senses, leaving her numb and empty.

After a long and terrible half-minute, he turned and looked coldly at her, surprised to find her still there, and annoyed that he should still be bothered by her presence.

'Have you nothing better to do?' he demanded irritably. 'Get out of my sight, Linnet, and for your own sake keep out of it as much as possible.'

CHAPTER NINE

THERE was nothing, Linnet discovered in the days to come, quite so saddening as knowing yourself to be mistrusted, the object of suspicion, barely tolerated by the one person in the world for whom you would cheerfully have walked over live coals.

Max had been cool and distant with her prior to the day he found the photographs, and in front of others he maintained a polite exterior. But sometimes Linnet would look up and find his eyes resting on her with a kind of thoughtful disbelief, and she longed to break through the barriers he had thrown up between them and persuade him he was wrong.

It wasn't possible. He had set his face so firmly against her that she knew she would get nowhere. She hardly saw him, and then only in the company of others, and he had given instructions that since he had a lot of work to do no one was to interrupt him in his study.

'As if I would; I have never done that!' Dina exclaimed indignantly to Linnet. 'Always I have respected that as his private place, and left him alone there. I cannot understand what is wrong with him lately.'

But I have tracked him down in his private place, Linnet thought, burning with shame and embarrassment. Those orders had been given specifically to deter her, to prevent her from seeking him out and pleading her case. He did not want to listen to her, did not want to see her more than he had to, or even to be reminded of her presence. She had not thought anyone could be so implacable once his mind was made up. Well, now she knew!

One day, when the air was crisp and cool, but the day sunny and free from the encroaching mists that plagued the city as autumn marched steadily towards winter, Linnet was on the sheltered patio with Cassie, who was bouncing her ball, glad to be partly outdoors after several days confined inside.

She watched the little girl fondly, thinking how she seemed to have put on a spurt of growth lately. She was going to be tall, as Max was—as Joanna had been—there was little doubt about it.

'*Ciao, bambina.*' Max's sudden appearance caused Linnet to stiffen apprehensively, but Cassie hurled herself at him, and then straightened up, more sedately, conscious of her increasing maturity.

'Papà—you must not call me that any more!' she reprimanded him. 'I am *not* a baby—I am a big girl, and will soon be going to school.'

She went back to bouncing her ball happily, and Linnet, aware of Max's eyes on her, did not flinch from meeting his sober gaze.

'She is certainly ready for school,' she said quietly. 'It will be good for her to be with other children.'

'I did not ask for your opinion, nor do I require it,' he said, his voice low, so that it did not carry across the patio to where Cassie played, but still so cold that it struck a chill to Linnet's heart. 'You are here only because, with the innocence of children, my daughter trusts you. If I had thought for a minute that her trust was misplaced, your bags would have been packed long ago.'

'I would never hurt Cassie in any way,' Linnet said indignantly.

He looked thoughtfully at her.

'I believe you would not,' he conceded, but the chill did not leave his eyes. 'And perhaps when she goes to school,' he added, 'she will begin to use the beautiful name she was given—Cosima—not the corruption my late wife made of it.'

'All children have pet names when they are small,' Linnet said. Even now, the reflex that had made her defend Joanna was not quite dead.

'Some of them are inapt and not very complimentary,' he replied smartly. 'My wife occasionally referred laughingly to a little "mouse" who so tiresomely followed her around. I suppose that was you. Didn't you ever object to that epithet?'

Linnet reddened, and a slow, painful tide flowed over her. Joanna had found her tiresome, her childish admiration amusing, had she? And he took pleasure in telling her that now, knowing that it would hurt. What he could not know, fortunately, was that the worst pain of all was caused by his desire to wound her, by the distaste and contempt he felt for her, which still could not extinguish her love for him.

'I don't know that I particularly cared for "songbird" but I put up with it,' she retorted tartly. 'Our great poet, Shakespeare, said, "What's in a name——?"'

'"That which we call a rose By any other name would smell as sweet,"' he completed promptly, and just for a second she surprised a fugitive sadness in his eyes. 'I'm not so sure. Nothing is ever what we think it is.'

She watched him go, and thought she could not sink any deeper into misery. His opinion of her was so low that there was no way she could redeem it. Nor could she prove that the Vernes had not sent her to spy on him; since obviously he did not trust them either, their denial, even if she could have obtained it, would mean nothing to him.

What hurt was not simply the fact that soon she would have to leave here, and never see him again. She had known that all along. You could not lose what was never yours, and she had steeled herself to accept that. No, by far the worst thing was to leave knowing that he thought badly of her, and always would—in so far as he would remember her at all.

The good memories—the lovely, sunlit day on Burano, the simple happiness of her birthday party, the moments of rapport and understanding—all these would count for nothing and be forgotten. She would leave only a legacy of resentment and mistrust behind her.

She was thankful for only one thing: he had not told anyone else what he had come to believe about her. Linnet would have read it in Dina's eyes, if he had, and in the changed attitude of the Ca' Favorita staff. He had spared her their censure and dislike, probably thinking that he had disarmed her himself simply by telling her what he knew. But when she had gone, would he tell them then that, according to him, the girl they had befriended had been no more than a paid snooper? Would they all hate her? And—oh, lord, would Cassie get to hear about it one day? Would Cassie hate her, too?

Linnet did not think she could bear it, but she knew, unhappily, that there was no real alternative, and so she dragged herself through those last days, smiling with feigned serenity and forcing herself to behave normally with people she had come to care for. Drinking in the beauty of Venice which never failed her, even now as the days grew colder and winter approached, she said a slow goodbye to it, for she did not think she could endure coming back here again. There were too many memories.

* * *

'The Danielis are coming for drinks tonight,' Max said one morning at breakfast, addressing himself ostensibly to Dina, and ignoring Linnet, as if it were none of her business. As, of course, it was not, she reminded herself miserably.

It was the kind of morning which depressed the spirits, rain driving against the windows and plopping noisily into the canals, grey skies, a chill damp seeping through the ancient fabric of the *palazzos*, despite the unobtrusive hum of central heating. Linnet had thought she could not feel more unhappy than she did, but now she knew she had been quite wrong. Tonight, Antonia would be here, sleek, dark and glowing, like a smoothly purring cat inspecting a new basket with a view to taking possession.

'Will they be staying to dinner?' she heard Dina asking, as she wrenched her gloomy thoughts back from future misery to present unhappiness.

'No, they are eating at the Cipriani. Antonia's brother, Paolo—you remember him?—has recently arrived back from Canada, and it is something of a celebration. But I have not seen him for some years, and apparently he has a new wife. Also there is some business he wants to interest me in.'

Linnet stirred her cappuccino restlessly, disturbing the froth. All pals together, she thought sourly. The whole family over for drinks, new relatives to be introduced, business links to be forged. A sure sign that in the near future, perhaps, the two families would be joined by marriage?

She wondered briefly if Antonia liked children—not just if she would love her own future offspring, but the child she would inherit. Well, it would not take much for her to be a better mother than Joanna had proved,

Linnet reflected. Did Cassie know and like Antonia? Had Max taken all this into consideration? Or would he, as he had the first time, simply do what he wanted, regardless?

'I think I had better go talk to Aldo about canapés,' Dina mused, after Max had left the table. 'And I really do believe we had better have champagne.'

Linnet cast her a quick glance.

'Aldo usually manages very well on his own, when people come for drinks,' she observed. 'Is there something special about this particular occasion?'

'Paolo Danieli is newly married, and we have not met his wife,' Dina said, somewhat evasively. 'The welcome must be suitable.'

Linnet was not fooled. She would have liked to ask Dina if there were any plans actually afoot between Max and Antonia, but she did not dare rush in, as once she might have done. Max's accusations had subtly changed her position in the household, and although no one else knew she was in disgrace she felt constrained and unable to be completely natural.

Besides, Max had been so withdrawn and secretive lately that it was possible Dina did not actually know what stage the relationship had reached, although obviously she was aware of its significance.

As the day progressed, Linnet dreamed up any number of reasons and excuses for not being present for drinks. The simplest and most obvious was to plead an impending cold or a headache, and skip dinner as well. There was sure to be talk about the Danielis, and she had no desire to listen to it. But more than anything else she did not want to be there for the cocktail ritual, alongside Antonia, and have her suspicions confirmed by her own eyes.

No one will miss me, she persuaded herself. No one will know that my excuses are fabricated. But would they? The only dignity she held on to was the relief of knowing that Max was unaware of the depth of her feelings for him. Certainly, he knew she had found him physically attractive, that she had been unable to deny or hide whenever he had touched her. But he did not know she loved him. If she did not put in an appearance, would his sharp mind make the connection and assume, all too rightly, that she was jealous?

Finally, even more than this sneaking fear, it was a hard core of stubbornness that would not let her take the easy way out. She would be there, she would smile and chat and sip her champagne, her every action declaring that she did not give a damn about Max di Angeli. He could marry whomever he chose. What was it to her? She would be going home soon, flying free of this golden cage forever.

She wore the cream dress she had worn on her birthday. The weather, of course, had turned considerably cooler since then, but once people arrived it would be warm enough, she thought hopefully, shivering slightly in the vast palatial drawing-room.

Dina noticed her shudder.

'*Dio mio*, no wonder you are cold—that dress is not warm enough for the evenings now!' she remonstrated. 'Why don't we go shopping for some more clothes for the cooler season?'

Linnet shrugged. 'It's hardly worthwhile,' she protested. 'I shall be going back to England soon, and I have a wardrobe of winter clothes there. Perhaps I should have brought a few with me, but I didn't think that far ahead.'

'Meanwhile you shiver,' Dina said reprovingly. 'You will catch a chill, Linnet, and that will be bad for your throat. Let me lend you a shawl.'

'No—truly, I'm warm enough,' Linnet insisted. She was not going to be inveigled into a shopping expedition with Dina, because the very last thing she intended doing was to spend any more of Max's money. It sat untouched in the bank, where it would remain. If he thought she was on someone else's payroll, then so be it. Between now and the time she left this house she would manage with what she had.

The caviare was best beluga, the smoked salmon was a brand Max had flown in regularly from Scotland, and the champagne was a *premier cuvée*. Everything was perfect, like a picture from a glossy magazine, Linnet thought, from the glow of the chandeliers drawing out the jewel colours of carpets and tapestries to the host himself, resplendent in his black velvet jacket.

Antonia wore deepest crimson, a shade her own colouring enabled her to carry off superbly. She looked perfectly at home in these elegant surroundings, and Linnet did not fail to notice that she made sure she was at Max's side most of the time, as if she were already the hostess. To his credit, he behaved always in a manner which accorded Dina this position, but the point was made nevertheless. The new crown princess had arrived!

Paolo Danieli was a handsome young man of about twenty-seven, whose dark good looks mirrored his sister's. He had hot, questing eyes which lingered on Linnet far too frequently for a man who had been married so short a time, especially as his Canadian bride, Beverley, was shy to the point of timidity, and obviously overwhelmed by the richness and splendour all around her.

Since her husband was not offering her anything like the support she needed on this important social outing in her new country, she had homed in eagerly on Linnet.

'The trouble is, I don't speak Italian,' she confided in a hesitant whisper. 'I wish I were fluent, like you.'

'You soon will be. I didn't know a great deal when I first came here, a few months ago,' Linnet said reassuringly. 'And, after all, you will have your husband to teach you.'

Beverley looked adoringly at Paolo, who was deep in discussion with Max, and then her doubts returned.

'I hope so,' she sighed. 'We are still more or less on our honeymoon, but Paolo is always talking to other people.'

'Well, if he's talking to Max, it will be business, so don't worry,' Linnet grinned.

'Oh, yes—Paolo works for Daddy, you know, and Daddy wants him to bring Signor di Angeli in on some deal,' Beverly said vaguely.

Daddy obviously being the chairman, it had done Paolo no harm to marry his daughter, Linnet thought cynically, feeling sorry for the shy girl, and hoping there was more to the marriage than blatant ambition.

Antonia's throaty laugh broke in on their conversation.

'Paolo and Max might have business other than electronics to discuss,' she hinted in Italian, then, seeing Beverley's blank look, switched to English and repeated what she had said. 'Especially since my father has now joined them,' she added.

'I'm sorry—I don't understand,' the Canadian girl whispered, clearly in awe of her elegant sister-in-law.

'Linnet will explain it to you,' Antonia laughed, and her amber eyes challenged Linnet's, a smile of malicious mischief playing around her shapely lips.

'I doubt it,' Linnet said, as equably as possible, 'since I haven't the faintest idea what you mean.'

It was a barefaced lie, of course. She knew very well what Antonia was insinuating. The men of the families had their heads together, and the subject of the discussion was a merger, but not of companies.

'I think you do,' Antonia said lightly.

And if she did? Linnet puzzled. Why was this stunningly beautiful, oddly devious Italian girl at pains to get her to admit it?

Antonia raised her delicately arched eyebrows meaningfully and turned her power-house smile full on Beverley, who shrank almost visibly.

'There will be changes in this household,' she said. 'Linnet, who is not so ingenuous as she pretends, is well aware of this.'

Linnet would have given a lot for a swift and foolproof escape from this gathering right then. But there did not seem to be any chance of finding one, so she said evenly, 'I'm not ingenuous, nor do I pretend to be. What you say may well be so, but since I shan't be here I'm not in a position to comment.'

'You will not be here?' Paolo had detached himself from Max and his father, and drifted over to join them, picking up Linnet's last words. 'I am desolated to hear this. Why must you run away so soon?'

He rested one hand on his wife's shoulder, which was quite permissible, and the other on Linnet's. Across the room, she intercepted a sudden glare of distaste from Max, but it wasn't this which made her carefully move a step away, disengaging the hand in doing so. She just did not like the way Paolo's eyes frankly and lustfully appraised her, regardless of the fact that his wife was right beside him. In fact, she did not like him at all.

To be honest, she did not care much for the Danielis as a clan. Signor Danieli had a dismissive way of sizing everyone up in terms of his or her financial or commercial importance, his wife had hard, acquisitive eyes and a haughty manner. As for Antonia——

She said, quite pleasantly, but maintaining a formal distance, 'It is not a matter of running away, *signore*——'

'Paolo,' he insisted, his eyes still intent on her. Linnet did not pick up the invitation.

'—I simply have to return to England to attend to business of my own.'

'Which is?' he persisted, sliding a surreptitious arm around her waist. 'What is it that you do, for which it is worth leaving La Serenissima?'

'I'm a student,' Linnet said shortly, fully intending to drop the subject right there.

Antonia emitted a low laugh.

'It is mysterious. We are given to understand that Linnet has trained to be an operatic singer,' she said lightly. 'Since we have never heard her sing, we have to take her claim on trust.'

Her tone was jesting, and to a casual listener could have been passed off as meaningless, cocktail-party banter. But there was a goading, mocking note hovering just beneath the surface levity which was as clear as a bell to Linnet's acute, musically trained ear. She was aware of a sudden stillness all around her, and it came to her, all at once, that she could not let this pass. She had no idea why Antonia had chosen to treat her as an adversary, but she knew that if it killed her, ruined her, or rendered her dumb for the rest of her days she must put this taunting woman in her place.

'I don't recall having made any such claim to you, *signorina*,' she replied quietly. 'But no matter. If you wish it, I will sing.'

Drawing herself up straight, clasping her hands lightly just below her ribcage, Linnet inhaled deeply, regularly, as she had been taught to do. And, as *it* had been taught to do, her voice responded. Into a room in which, all of a sudden, a pin could have been dropped, and been heard resoundingly, she gave them the beautiful Mozart aria '*Voi che sapete*'. Every note was as clear and true as a bell, every syllable precisely phrased—and more. The whole of her yearning heart, which could find no other channel for its suffering, translated into beauty and expressed, perfectly, through the music. Linnet sang, and her predominantly Italian audience stood silenced into reverence until the very end.

The silence lingered even after the last notes died away, and Linnet was acutely conscious that every pair of eyes was trained on her. But she didn't care about the smouldering admiration in Paolo's, or Signora Danieli's astonished appreciation. Even the grim satisfaction of having called Antonia's bluff and rendered her speechless, for once, did not give her the pleasure she might have expected.

The only reaction that truly mattered to her was Max's, and on his face she saw such a thunderous fury, laced with such a deep and bitter disillusionment that she actually felt all her internal organs contract with fear, simply from meeting his gaze. She did not understand this furious displeasure, but she shrank from it nevertheless.

It was Dina who broke the astounded silence, clapping her hands together enthusiastically.

'*Bravissima*!' she exclaimed. 'That was beautiful—beautiful, Linnet! You have a rare gift!'

Yes—for making a complete fool of myself, Linnet thought, staring blindly around her at the circle of faces. Whatever had possessed her to do such a crazy thing?

'Excuse me!' she choked, and without a backward glance ran headlong from the room, not stopping until she reached her bedroom and slammed the door behind her.

Darkness had fallen, but she did not switch on the light. She sat on her bed, motionless, for what could have been five minutes or could have been half an hour. She had no way of knowing.

Two thoughts reverberated in her head, circling round and round relentlessly. One was, I sang, the other, Max hates me.

Her voice was there, as pure and clear as ever, as technically capable as it had been before her illness. She was out of practice, but even that had not prevented her from reaching out for the high notes with assurance; it had not taken away the richness of texture, nor the perfection of timing that was as much instinct as training. As a singer, she was not finished.

As a woman, she undoubtedly was. The way Max had looked at her told her beyond question how much he despised her. She had thought she could sink no lower in his estimation than she already had, but somehow what she had done tonight had put the final seal on any lingering hope she had nursed of partially redeeming herself in his eyes. Why, she did not know, but she had seen it.

The brisk, peremptory knock on the door was no more than a formality. It was opened at once, without a pause for her to give permission to enter, and Max stood there, framed by the light from the corridor. He was perfectly calm now, but she knew him well enough to realise that this uncanny stillness presaged his worst anger, and she quailed inwardly.

But she neither moved nor spoke as he came in, closing the door behind him. Now the only light in the room was that filtering through the open curtains, and since it was a black, moonless night this was reduced to the occasional gleam from another lighted window in the darkness beyond.

'I hope you are well satisfied with your bravura performance down there.' His voice cut the silence with cold, knife-like precision.

Linnet shrugged.

'It proves I can still sing,' she said defiantly.

'It proves you have about as much reasoning power as the creature you are named after,' he said contemptuously. 'Didn't your specialist expressly say you were not to sing? Not that, by this stage, you would be unable to, but that you *must not*. Didn't you pause to consider what damage you might do to your vocal cords by exercising them prematurely?'

She stared at him through the gloom, puzzled by the force of his anger.

'I didn't think of it,' she admitted, taken aback. The truth was, she hadn't thought at all, and even if she had she might still, in her indignation, have gone ahead and done exactly the same. She had behaved with total irresponsibility, goaded on by jealousy of the woman who was about to claim the man *she* loved.

'You—didn't—think,' he repeated, laying equal, scornful emphasis on each word. 'One day, that will be your epitaph, Linnet: "She did not think".'

'Very amusing,' she said. 'I really don't see why you are so het up—it's *my* voice, after all, and *my* business what I do with it. Hadn't you better get back to your...guests?'

'They've gone,' he said shortly. 'For one thing, they had a dinner engagement. For another, your little act was hard to follow.'

He took three steps towards her, and the power and anger flowing from him were truly alarming. Linnet sprang to her feet, but the bed was behind her, preventing her from backing away.

'You senseless, capricious little fool!' he flung at her, his voice hard and driven. 'You might have got away with it, and I hope, for your sake, you have. But you don't deserve to, if you can put at risk years of training, your own career, and the future pleasure of thousands simply for a frivolous desire to show off!'

'I wasn't showing off!' she denied hotly. 'I was provoked.'

'Oh, yes? By whom—by what?'

Linnet bit her lip. She could not drag Antonia into this without betraying why she had been so incensed by the girl's taunts, but Max was scarcely concerned, and his question was purely rhetorical.

'Provoked? Yes, I'm sure,' he drawled, his voice dripping sarcasm. 'When I referred to your performance, I did not mean only the singing. Do you think no one saw you making an exhibition of yourself with Paolo Danieli—encouraging him to paw you and undress you with his eyes? In *my* house, Linnet, under *my* roof, and with a man who has been married less than a month! Haven't you any shame?'

'Stop! Stop! Stop!' she shouted furiously, her voice hoarse with emotion. She did not have to endure this!

First he accused her of being a paid spy, and now he had the nerve to say that she had been leading on that awful Paolo!

'Why should I?' he demanded roughly. 'Obviously you are ripe for that sort of action, and have been for some time! Well, you don't have to seduce my guests. You only have to say. There's an easier remedy.'

In one swift action he shrugged his arms from the velvet jacket and flung it carelessly on the floor. His hand ripped at the bow-tie at his neck, discarding it viciously. Linnet's eyes widened, horrified, but already he had grasped her by the shoulders, pushing aside the loosely draped neckline of the cream dress to bare her neck and throat easily.

'No!' she cried, struggling under his hands. 'No, I don't want——'

'But you do want, Linnet, and that's half your trouble,' he said, his voice thick with purpose. He was formidably strong in his anger, and she could find no escape as his hard mouth descended on hers, taking rough and peremptory possession.

And then . . . somehow, it was as if all the anger was emptied out of him in that one long, furious kiss. He drew back from her, briefly, and through the half-light they gazed at each other with eyes full of questions, caught in a moment from which they could no longer retreat.

Reaching out, he ran an exploratory finger along the line of her neck and down to the swell of her breast. She shivered, the beginnings of a sob caught in her throat, but she did not protest. It was useless. They were here together, however it had come to be, and there was no longer any question of refusing or denying the need in her. Not only was she unresisting as his hands dealt with the tie at the back of her dress, and her minimal underwear, her own fingers were already at work on the buttons of his shirt. Without a word they helped one another until they were both naked on the bed, without a word, he took her in his arms, and the night exploded around them.

For so long she had wanted him to make love to her that her joy and eagerness quite made up for her lack of experience. He had come to her in anger, but now, holding her, touching her, he was tender but purposeful, leading her, showing her, inviting her to meet him in pleasure, so that each caress drew her inevitably to the next, and nothing they did together was wrong, nothing jarred or was out of place, or without its own special delight.

It was like music, she thought, symphonic, lyric, each note, each chord a part of the whole, and inseparable from it. And, like music, soaring to a climax that was right and inevitable, and so beautiful that it almost brought her to tears. She lay serene in his arms, washed up on a peaceful shore she had thought never to reach, and drifted off into the deepest, most blissful sleep of her life.

She never felt him leave her, and only waking suddenly, abruptly, became shockingly aware that she was alone beneath the white lace coverlet. Sitting up swiftly, she stared around her. It was still dark, still night, but what her waking senses had instinctively known was easily confirmed. He had gone. There was no trace of him in the room, no evidence of his having been there. Only her naked body and deliciously bruised lips reminded her of the completeness of her own surrender.

The peace, the rightness she had felt falling asleep in his arms had vanished like a mirage, and in its place a dark, angry despair began to wash over her. It had seemed so perfect while they were making love, and because she loved and desired him she had allowed herself to believe that it was so.

Now, in the stark, lonely aftermath, she remembered the reasons which had brought him to her room in the first place. Anger, contempt, disgust. He thought she had been making a play for Paolo, and he had wanted to teach her a lesson. No matter that he had then proceeded to make love to her with great delicacy and enjoyment. He was a man of some experience, and knew not only how to ensure his own pleasure, but hers, too. If he set out to seduce a woman, he would do it properly, thoroughly, so that she would remember it forever, and no future lover would ever quite be able to erase the memory, or supersede it.

And that's what he has done to me, Linnet thought bitterly. He has made sure that I am unfit for any other man, that I won't ever be able to love another man, and if I were foolish enough to try the ghost of this night would always rise between us. Max had taken a fearful revenge on her for the wrong he believed she had done him, and that was all the brief enjoyment of her body had meant to him. He didn't care—not a hoot. If he had cared, he would not have left her alone, sneaking off like a successful thief. If he had cared, even a little, he would still be here.

CHAPTER TEN

DISTRAUGHT and unhappy as she was, Linnet was sure of one thing beyond a suspicion of doubt. She could not stay here in the Ca' Favorita, not even for what remained of this night. Not even for another hour. After what had happened between them, she could not bear to see Max again, to face the grim triumph in his eyes, his certainty that he had broken her will, taken her, and that she was now his to discard.

Very quietly, but mechanically, like a robot, she dressed in jeans and her warmest sweater, and without care for how they would emerge at the other end stuffed clothes and possessions into her suitcase. Whatever would not go in, she left behind.

Her watch told her it was just after two a.m. The household would be asleep, and there was no way of getting out by the front door without rousing Gianni. But she thought she could slip out quietly the back way, and at least until morning no one would know she had gone.

Only the dim lights which glowed all night illuminated the corridors as she crept quietly along them and down the stairs, in terror of actually meeting someone and having to explain herself. But all was quiet; there were no insomniacs on the prowl, and no light glowed from beneath the door of Max's study. At the back door, she slid the big iron bolt and turned the key, then stepped out into the night.

The alleys were dark and eerie and she walked along, stepping as briskly as she could while carrying her suitcase. There was no one about, and she let out an involuntary scream as something soft brushed against her leg. But a sharp hiss and a pair of malevolent amber eyes gleaming in the darkness reassured her that it was only a cat on its nocturnal wanderings, and she continued on her way. There was little chance of her picking up a passing water-taxi on the smaller canals, but she reckoned she could get one at the Rialto.

Likewise flights. She had not stopped to risk using the telephone, therefore she had not been able to reserve a seat, nor did she know how soon there would be a flight to England. It didn't matter. The earliest one out would do, even if she had to change to another flight somewhere else. What mattered was never to see Max di Angeli again, and to hell with his contract. He could sue her through every court in Europe if he so wished, but she would not live under his roof.

She was sorry if Cassie was disappointed, but persuaded herself that the little girl would soon forget her. Before leaving she had taken a minute to write her a short note.

> Dear Cassie—I have to go back to England in a hurry. Please look after Paddington for me. He's too big to go in my case. Be good at your new school, and have fun. Lots of love—your friend, Linnet.

More she could not explain to her. More Cassie would not understand until, one day, she herself became a woman. Dear Cassie—I'm leaving because your father has broken my heart irreparably? No. For now, this would have to suffice.

If Linnet's parents were surprised when she turned up midway through a raw November morning, they did not make a fuss. It was obvious that their daughter was in a dreadful state; she looked tired and unwell, was tight-lipped and wooden, and needed a hot bath, hot soup, and sleep, in that order. Despite the lunchtime rush in the bar and kitchen, Linnet's mother soon had her tucked up in bed with hot-water bottles at her feet, the curtains drawn, and the heating turned up.

She did not think she would sleep, but exhaustion won its inevitable victory. The flight had been a nightmare, but not even the turbulence in the air had been able to dislodge the frozen numbness around her heart.

Max—he had punished her terribly for misdeeds she had not committed, and yet she still loved him. And she had given herself to him completely—yes, because in the end he had not used force. He had not needed to.

It was going to take her a long time to get over him, if she ever could. But when she woke up, after sleeping through the rest of the day and the night that followed it, she had come to a decision, made, perhaps, by her unconscious mind while she slept.

Life went on. It had to. Going into a decline because one's heart was broken was all very well in Victorian novelettes, but it would not do for twentieth-century reality. Yes, she loved a man who not only could never be hers, but who despised her thoroughly, but even if she could not forget she must go forward—see the specialist, complete her training. She did not think she had done any irreparable damage to her throat when she'd sung at the Ca' Favorita, and now it was all she had left to live for.

She got up, pulled the curtains, put on her jeans and a clean sweater, and with a determined smile on her face went down to the kitchen, where her mother, having just finished serving the guests' breakfasts, was sitting down with a well-earned cup of tea. Her father, she guessed, would be stocking up the shelves in the bar, so for the moment the two women were alone.

'Well, you certainly must have needed that sleep,' her mother said affectionately, but with worry still lurking in her eyes as she regarded her daughter. 'How are you feeling now?'

'Fine. Hungry,' said Linnet. 'No—you sit down. I'll make some toast. But if there's tea left in the pot I'd love a cup.'

'There's plenty. I've just made it.' She watched as Linnet busied herself with toast and marmalade. 'We weren't expecting you back until just before Christmas, and obviously something's wrong. Do you want to talk about it?'

Linnet shook her head gently.

'Not yet,' she said. The pain was still too sharp to bring out into the open and examine, and there were areas she was sure she could never discuss with anyone, not even her mother. 'Let's just say there were difficulties, and I decided I had to leave.'

She poured the tea and squared up, adopting a deliberately bright manner. 'So here I am, and I might as well make myself useful. I'll do a turn behind the bar at lunchtime, if you like.'

Her mother was doubtful.

'We *are* short-staffed, but... I don't know. Don't you need the rest?'

'No. I've had enough rest. I need the activity,' Linnet said firmly. Anything was preferable to moping about, brooding.

And so she spent the morning and early afternoon helping her father in the bar, and since it was a busy session she did not have time to think, which suited her down to the ground. I'll be all right, I *will*, she told herself, ignoring the persistent ache below her ribs.

The rush had eased off, and the bar had almost emptied, when to Linnet's astonishment Rupert walked in. The sight of him gave her a sharp shock, bringing back thoughts of Joanna, which led inevitably to thoughts of Max.

'Linnet,' he said, with a rather wan smile, and she realised that the memories were still bad for him, too.

'Rupert! I didn't know you were round these parts,' she said carefully, wondering how much he knew about her own recent past.

'I'm not—I'm simply passing through, and I couldn't resist stopping by the village,' he said wryly. 'I haven't actually been back since the... since the funeral. Pour me half a pint of lager, there's a good girl. I'm trying to pluck up courage to visit the Vernes. Trouble is, Lady V. scares me witless, and always did! So how's the music?'

She stared at him. 'Didn't you know? I was ill, and had to give it up for a year. Hopefully, I shall be able to start my training again soon.'

He shook his head. 'Sorry... I know I saw you at the funeral, but I really wasn't taking anything in at that time. And Jo hadn't told me anything about it.'

'You saw her? Before the... ?' Her voice dried up at the look of anguish on the young man's face. '*I'm* sorry, Rupert. We won't talk about it if you'd rather not. I know that you and she were once fond of one another, but it was a long time ago.'

He set down his glass and looked bleakly at her. They were alone now, in the bar, her father having disappeared down the cellar, but even so Rupert's voice was very quiet as he said, 'It wasn't a long time ago, Linnet. Joanna and I were lovers—up until the day she died.'

Linnet's sense of shock was so deep that she could hardly move. Only her fingers played aimlessly with a drip-mat on the bar, and her words came out as a whisper.

'I had no idea.'

'But I always loved her,' he said. 'When we were younger, I thought we would marry. But I wasn't good enough for her then, according to the Vernes. When she met that wealthy, aristocratic Italian they were over the moon, because he was such a great catch. True, she was briefly crazy about him, but that might have burned itself out if they hadn't pushed and encouraged her into marriage.'

Linnet was silent, still wrestling with the astonishment dealt her by his revelations, and he sighed.

'So off she went in this big romantic cloud, and got married, had a kid... I didn't see her again until we met by chance a couple of years ago, in St Tropez. We started seeing each other secretly, whenever we could. She didn't mind the intrigue, but I hated it! I wanted her permanently.'

Joanna had ranted and raved about Max's philanderings, while all the time it was she who had been conducting a long-term affair! Linnet bit her lip as the last of the scales fell from her eyes.

'She told *me* that her husband was two-timing her consistently,' she said bitterly.

'Jo believed what it suited her to believe,' he said quietly. 'Even though I loved her I had no illusions. I knew what she was like! Telling herself that he was unfaithful removed her own guilt for what she was doing, you see. I wanted her to get a divorce and marry me. She said he would never allow it, but I don't think she ever really wanted to give up the luxurious lifestyle he could give her.'

'But she left him in the end,' Linnet said. 'When she came back to England.'

'She didn't leave him. He had found out about us, so she ran away to escape facing the music,' Rupert said drily. 'Apparently he has a formidable temper. She thought that once he had cooled off she could go back to her jet-setting and her designer clothes...and I would still be there in the background, whenever she wanted me.

'I'd had enough of it, Linnet. I gave her an ultimatum—either she got a divorce and married me, or it was all over between us. That's when she jumped into her car and drove off in a rage, and... well, you know the rest.'

'How awful for you,' Linnet said with fierce sympathy, putting her hand lightly over his. He gripped her fingers with unexpected strength.

'I knew she had been drinking heavily. I shouldn't have pushed her,' he said brokenly. 'It was *all* my fault, Linnet. *I* killed her.'

'No!' she said urgently. 'You mustn't think that. Who can say why things happen as they do? The chain of coincidences, of ifs and buts, is too long, too complicated. And Joanna herself must bear an equal responsibility, in the end.'

She was not sure she had convinced him, but he gave a weak smile and pressed her hand before leaving. One day, if he ever came this way again, perhaps she would tell him a little about her time in Italy, about Cassie...but not now. The memories were still too painful, for both of them.

Outside, the greyness had lifted and a watery sun was struggling through the clouds. Linnet put on her sheepskin jacket and warm boots and trudged out, stepping briskly along the country lanes and up the familiar downland path that brought her, finally, to a spot from where she could look down on the village, the neat pattern of farms all around it, and Verne Hall on the outskirts.

You must not blame yourself, she had told Rupert, and she had meant it. The laws that governed all their lives were too complex for them fully to understand. If Joanna had not gone to that gala ball in Paris . . . if Lady Verne had not been so eager to pull off an ambitious marriage for her daughter...if Max had not been at loggerheads with his own father, and hell-bent on proving that he could please himself. And maybe Joanna, restless, unstable and impossible to satisfy, was born to wreak havoc in the lives of others. Whose was the right to sit in judgement and apportion blame?

But that was what *she* had done, when she'd gone out to Venice with the fires of anger in her heart, so obstinately sure that the responsibility lay firmly at Max di Angeli's door. It had taken her several hard, self-critical months to learn that nothing was that clear-cut, but not until this day had she grasped the full extent of her misjudgement of him.

If, in the end, he had got the wrong idea about her and about her motives, it was only because she, initially, had done the same. Her deception had rebounded on her. Well, I paid a high price, she thought soberly as she turned and began the descent back towards the village.

Her mother met her in the hotel's small lobby as she came in, and her face wore a bemused, concerned expression.

'You have a visitor,' she said.

'I do?' Linnet frowned. 'But I only arrived yesterday, and nobody knows I'm here.'

'Mr di Angeli does,' her mother replied bluntly. 'He's in the private sitting-room. I gave him coffee and told him I didn't know where you were, but that I didn't think you would be out long.'

Max—here? Sensations of panic threatened to swamp Linnet, and she glanced wildly around, as if searching for an escape route. If Max had come here, *he* would not be 'passing through'. He was not that kind of man!

'I don't want to see him,' she said firmly.

'My dear, I don't think you have a choice,' her mother said gently. 'He made it very plain he isn't going to go away until he *has* seen you, so you might as well get it over with.'

'But you don't understand!' Linnet cried.

'Better than you think, my girl,' her mother replied, smiling into her daughter's stricken face. 'I can see you're in love with him, and, although you haven't told me much, obviously that has to do with why you landed on us so suddenly. Now—he's come all this way in pursuit of you...and I must say I like him. He seems very charming and civilised...and sincere. Don't you think you should sort out your differences?'

Linnet groaned. Her mother believed this was simply a lovers' tiff, that she and Max would fall into each other's arms, and all would be well. If only it were true! If only it were that simple!

'You don't know Max,' she said grimly. 'I broke my contract when I came home, and he doesn't like to be crossed. He's probably here to slap a writ on me, or whatever the procedure is.'

'In person?' her mother said drily. 'I thought lawyers did that. Run along. I shall only be in the kitchen, but you're a big girl, now, and I doubt you'll need me. And take those muddy boots off first,' she added.

Linnet removed the boots and hung her coat in the cupboard. Her reflection in the long hall mirror showed the heightened colour in her cheeks that could have been caused by the cold outdoors, but was more likely a result of her warring emotions.

How could she face him? If he had followed her from Venice simply to berate her for running out on him before she was legally entitled to—and she could think of no other reason for him to be here—her own feelings were far more complicated. Merely to see him would remind her, inevitably, of the passionate hour she had spent with him in her bedroom at the Ca' Favorita, and she knew, no matter what he felt about her, that the sight of him could not help but revive her desire.

But her mother was undoubtedly right. He would not go away, and I, she told herself, drawing up her slender form as straight and tall as possible, have stopped running. It was time to take the bull by the horns. Taking a deep breath, she turned her back on the mirror and stepped briskly towards the sitting-room.

He was standing by the window which overlooked the gardens, and in complete contrast to their indeterminate winter drabness he seemed to glow, to bring the room alive with the tanned warmth of his face, the vivid black of his hair and the deep, unforgettable blue of his eyes. His fine wool overcoat was carelessly slung over the back of a chair, his flight bag lay discarded on the floor. Only as she looked at him more closely, her heart reliving the desperately longed-for touch and feel of him, did she observe the hint of strain and tiredness in the lines either side of his mouth. Once before she had seen him look like that, after an emergency journey and a sleepless night. Surely her misdemeanours did not merit the same effect?

Across the room she met his eyes steadily, looking for anger, for contempt . . . at the very least for stinging disapproval. She found none of these, but she could not identify exactly what it was she read in his expression. He was not smiling, precisely, but there was a faint curve to his lips, and his voice, when he spoke, was softly purposeful.

'You were not too hard to hunt down, songbird. If you had wanted to run away from me, you should have found a safer hiding-place.'

'I did not imagine you would want to hunt me down,' she said quietly. Closing the door behind her, she turned to face him again. 'Before you start on me, Max, there's something I want to say that I should have said long ago, and it's this. I was wrong about you—about you and Joanna. I thought everything was your fault, that you cheated on her and made her unhappy, that your unfaithfulness drove her to her death. I know now that it wasn't true. I think I guessed it a long time ago, but I was too stubborn to admit I had made a mistake. I also realise now that she was the unfaithful one, after all. I'm sorry.'

His laughter was low and gently amused.

'I appreciate that must have been hard for you to say, Linnet, but you can stop metaphorically knocking your head on the floor now,' he said, and his gently sardonic humour made Linnet almost choke on her difficult confession. 'I wonder how you reached the conclusion that Joanna was playing away, as they say? Certainly, I never told you.'

'No, but Rupert did. He was in here earlier this morning, and told me the whole story.'

'Ah.' She had thought, by rushing in with her admission, to do two things—to ease her conscience, which had long troubled her on this score, and to take the wind out of his sails. If she had succeeded with the first objective, she had failed dismally with the second. He did not seem at all concerned, and she did not know what to make of him.

'Let the past lie,' he said dismissively. 'I did make Joanna unhappy, no doubt, for all I was, technically at least, faithful to her, and she made me equally miserable. I married her for all the wrong reasons, and I expect she did the same. By the time we realised it, there was Cosima...'

He suddenly gave an impatient shrug and took two paces forward, so that they were within touching-distance. Linnet's body felt as weak and insubstantial as straw, but it wasn't fear which drained her strength—it was need. She would not have cared at that moment if he shook her, or struck her, just so long as she felt the touch of his hands again.

'Let's stop playing these games, Linnet!' he exclaimed fiercely. 'I did not come all this way to talk about Joanna, and you know it!'

He was too close, too overwhelmingly male, and much too dear to her, and her control snapped.

'Forget it, Max!' she said tersely. 'You can take me all the way to the European Court of Justice if you like! You can take every penny I have or am likely to earn in the future, but I am not coming back to work out the last weeks of my contract! Wild horses could not drag me! You made your feelings for me only too plain!'

And now he did indeed reach out and seize her by the shoulders, not shaking her, but gripping her so hard that she could not move.

'Yes, I did, didn't I?' he demanded, in a voice wrung out with bitterness. 'And you threw them in my face! How can a woman lie in your arms and give herself with such sweetness...such apparent pleasure...and then up and run out on you in the middle of the night? That's what I want to know, Linnet! Did it really mean what I thought it meant, or nothing at all? *That's* what I have to find out, and there's only one way I can do so!'

He crushed her to him, his mouth on hers, his arms so tightly around her that it was difficult for her to breathe, but she was past caring, and her response was beyond reason—it was the response of her body and her heart. Her own arms went round his neck, her fingers caught in the thickness of his hair. Her eyes closed and she clung to him, living for nothing but the moment in his arms.

Slowly, at last, he raised his head and relaxed his arms, still keeping her fast in their circle.

'I didn't dream it, then?' he said, his voice hoarse with emotion. 'You did want me, Linnet? That, at least, was real.'

She was too shaken to attempt denial.

'It was real,' she confessed. 'How could I have pretended? Max, you must know that you were the first...that I hadn't given myself lightly. But then, when

I woke up, you had gone. I felt used . . . what was I supposed to think?'

His smile was tender now.

'What *did* you think, foolish songbird?'

'Why. . . that you had only intended to punish me for my deception... as you thought of it. Although you were wrong. What I did was crazy, but I was never in the pay of the Vernes, or anyone else.'

He said, 'I left you because I had already absented myself for so long that it was beginning to look embarrassing. I had to invent some nonsensical story for Dina about your not being well. Later, when I looked in, you were sleeping so peacefully I hadn't the heart to disturb you. I thought we would talk in the morning.

'As for your deception,' he went on, as Linnet, suddenly wide-eyed and speechless, gazed up at him, 'in the morning, when I found you had gone, I was pretty furious. I told Dina what I had suspected about you, and she, with her good sense, told me not to be such an idiot, that you were not the kind of girl who would stoop to such behaviour. I knew at once that she was right, that emotion had blinded me. *Love* had blinded me, Linnet, but now love has opened my eyes again, and I see clearly what you really are—a bright, true spirit who brought light to my darkness.'

Linnet choked, went pink, then pale again, her throat dry, her hands shaking, for this was a declaration of love such as she could not believe she was hearing.

'Max . . . don't go on . . . not unless you're sure it's the truth!' she gasped. 'Are you . . . are you really telling me that you love me?'

He groaned. 'I am trying my level best, *carissima*! Why do you think I was so angry when I heard you risking your beautiful voice just, as I thought, to impress that idiot Paolo?'

'It wasn't to impress Paolo, it was to impress Antonia!' Linnet cried. 'I was so jealous of her. I thought you loved her, that you were going to marry her! She certainly thinks so! So does Dina.'

His smile was grim.

'Not now, she doesn't,' he said. 'You don't think she actually believed my excuse for going missing for so long? As for Antonia—not that I wanted another playgirl for a wife—I virtually pushed her out of the door. She was well aware something was going on. You and I, my love, are probably gossip fodder for the whole of Venice by now.'

She heard the tender, teasing note in his voice, felt the strength of his arms around her, and saw, above all, the look of love in his eyes.

'Come back and marry me, Linnet, otherwise I shan't be able to hold up my head!' he grinned. 'Dina will be pleased, I know, and Cosima will be ecstatic, but it would make no difference to me if the whole world were against us. I've waited so long for you to stop seeing me as a villain—for you to admit to me, and to yourself, that you love me. Say it, Linnet. I can't wait any longer.'

For answer, she reached up and kissed him, long and thoroughly.

'*Ti amo*,' she said simply. 'I've loved you for a long time, Max. I fought it, told myself it couldn't be... but it did no good. I love you.'

He folded her and rocked her in his arms.

'We'll have a short engagement, for the sake of propriety,' he said. 'Then we'll see your specialist. Maestro Donetti can come to Venice to teach you—I'll make it worth his while. I don't want to confine you, dearest.

Only to love you. This marriage is for the rest of our lives.'

Linnet, secure and happy in the circle of his arms, had no doubts. Love was not a cage. It was a bright garden into which she freely flew, and would willingly stay—even if, sometimes, rain fell and clouds veiled the sun... So long as he shared it with her.

Some time later, Linnet's mother softly opened the door and peeped in, but her daughter and the handsome Italian did not see her. They were wrapped in each other's arms.

'I knew it would be all right,' she said with satisfaction as she closed the door and tiptoed quietly away.

PENNY
JORDAN
Lingering
Shadows

Next Month's Romances

Each month you can choose from a wide variety of romance with Mills & Boon. Below are the new titles to look out for next month, why not ask either Mills & Boon Reader Service or your Newsagent to reserve you a copy of the titles you want to buy – just tick the titles you would like and either post to Reader Service or take it to any Newsagent and ask them to order your books.

Please save me the following titles:	Please tick	√
SIMPLY IRRESISTIBLE	Miranda Lee	
HUNTER'S MOON	Carole Mortimer	
AT ODDS WITH LOVE	Betty Neels	
A DANGEROUS MAGIC	Patricia Wilson	
TOWER OF SHADOWS	Sara Craven	
THE UNMARRIED BRIDE	Emma Goldrick	
SWEET BETRAYAL	Helen Brooks	
COUNTERFEIT LOVE	Stephanie Howard	
A TEMPORARY AFFAIR	Kate Proctor	
SHADES OF SIN	Sara Wood	
RUTHLESS STRANGER	Margaret Mayo	
BITTERSWEET LOVE	Cathy Williams	
CAPTIVE BRIDE	Rosemary Carter	
WILLING OR NOT	Liza Hadley	
MASTER OF NAMANGILLA	Mons Daveson	
LOVE YOUR ENEMY	Ellen James	
A FOOLISH HEART	Laura Martin	

If you would like to order these books in addition to your regular subscription from Mills & Boon Reader Service please send £1.80 per title to: Mills & Boon Reader Service, Freepost, P.O. Box 236, Croydon, Surrey, CR9 9EL, quote your Subscriber No:................................ (If applicable) and complete the name and address details below. Alternatively, these books are available from many local Newsagents including W.H.Smith, J.Menzies, Martins and other paperback stockists from 13 August 1993.

Name:..

Address:...

....Post Code:.........................

To Retailer: If you would like to stock M&B books please contact your regular book/magazine wholesaler for details.

You may be mailed with offers from other reputable companies as a result of this application. If you would rather not take advantage of these opportunities please tick box ☐